All Brynn could think of was how much she was attracted to Rand, from his thick brown hair to the tips of his Gucci loafers

And especially everything in between.

Rand gave her a look that made her suddenly hot. "It's been such a great day that I don't want it to end. Come to River Walk with us."

No way, her mind was screaming, but her reply came from her heart. "I'd love to."

His face lit up like Fourth of July fireworks, his delight so obvious Brynn had to look away. She restrained herself from beating her hand against the window in frustration. Why hadn't she just said no?

Because Rand Benedict is a very special man, maybe the one you've been looking for all your life, a voice inside her head insisted.

But she hadn't been looking for a man, not even a special one.

Had she?

Dear Reader,

In the words of an ancient Chinese saying, we live in interesting times. Due to tumultuous world events, we appreciate more than ever security, solace, acceptance and love as bulwarks against the troubles of the day. In my series A PLACE TO CALL HOME, I've created a small town in upstate South Carolina, where love and acceptance, along with only occasional mayhem, abound. For the residents of Pleasant Valley, friends are family, and family is everything.

In *Spring in the Valley*, book three of the series, Officer Brynn Sawyer, one of Pleasant Valley's finest, finds her heart and values shaken by Yankee stranger Rand Benedict, a lawyer on a secret mission to the South. But Brynn has always given as good as she gets, and Rand soon discovers his life and expectations upended after being ticketed by the curvaceous cop.

I hope you'll enjoy the romantic skirmish between Brynn and Rand, aided by Rand's adorable nephew and ward, and as we say in the South, y'all come back and visit Pleasant Valley again early in 2006.

Happy reading!

Charlotte Douglas

CHARLOTTE DOUGLAS
Spring in the Valley

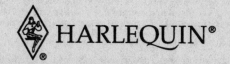

HARLEQUIN®

TORONTO • NEW YORK • LONDON
AMSTERDAM • PARIS • SYDNEY • HAMBURG
STOCKHOLM • ATHENS • TOKYO • MILAN • MADRID
PRAGUE • WARSAW • BUDAPEST • AUCKLAND

If you purchased this book without a cover you should be aware that this book is stolen property. It was reported as "unsold and destroyed" to the publisher, and neither the author nor the publisher has received any payment for this "stripped book."

ISBN 0-373-75065-X

SPRING IN THE VALLEY

Copyright © 2005 by Charlotte Douglas.

All rights reserved. Except for use in any review, the reproduction or utilization of this work in whole or in part in any form by any electronic, mechanical or other means, now known or hereafter invented, including xerography, photocopying and recording, or in any information storage or retrieval system, is forbidden without the written permission of the publisher, Harlequin Enterprises Limited, 225 Duncan Mill Road, Don Mills, Ontario M3B 3K9, Canada.

All characters in this book have no existence outside the imagination of the author and have no relation whatsoever to anyone bearing the same name or names. They are not even distantly inspired by any individual known or unknown to the author, and all incidents are pure invention.

This edition published by arrangement with Harlequin Books S.A.

® and TM are trademarks of the publisher. Trademarks indicated with ® are registered in the United States Patent and Trademark Office, the Canadian Trade Marks Office and in other countries.

www.eHarlequin.com

Printed in U.S.A.

ABOUT THE AUTHOR

The major passions of Charlotte Douglas's life are her husband—her high school sweetheart to whom she's been married for over three decades—and writing compelling stories. A national bestselling author, she enjoys filling her books with love of home and family, special places and happy endings. With their two cairn terriers, she and her husband live most of the year on Florida's central west coast, but spend the warmer months at their North Carolina mountaintop retreat.

No matter what time of year, readers can reach her at charlottedouglas1@juno.com. She's always delighted to hear from them.

Books by Charlotte Douglas

†A Place to Call Home
*Identity Swap

Chapter One

Officer Brynn Sawyer was definitely out of uniform. At the rate her friends were getting married, she contemplated with a wry chuckle, a bridesmaid's dress was beginning to feel like her backup wardrobe.

Recalling Jodie Nathan and Jeff Davidson's wedding earlier that day, she couldn't help smiling as she drove her SUV down the dark, winding road toward the valley highway. Hours ago, she and a few hundred other guests had given the happy couple a great send-off for their Bermuda honeymoon.

After most of the others had departed the festivities at Archer Farm, Brynn had remained behind to help the staff and clients clean up at the juvenile rehabilitation center that the groom had founded. The teenage boys, most of whom she knew well, both through personal encounters and from memorizing their rap sheets, had had other ideas. Refusing her offers of assistance, they had settled her in a deep chair in front of the great room fireplace, slipped a hassock under her high-heel-clad feet and placed a mug of hot chocolate in her hands. Then, insisting they were used to grunt work, they'd ordered her not to muss her pretty dress. In less than a year, Jeff Davidson and his staff of former Marines had worked miracles with their sixteen at-risk boys.

Contemplating Jeff and Jodie's well-earned happiness, Brynn drove slowly through the darkness. The only illumination on the narrow road was the high beams, and the only interior light came from the faint glow from the control panel. She briefly fingered a fold of her dress before taking hold of the wheel again. The full-length gown *was* pretty, as the teens had said, a delicate leaf-green silk, perfect for the first day of spring and new beginnings, and to complement the midnight-blue of her eyes.

"You're next," Jodie had declared after Brynn caught the bridal bouquet of apple blossoms, paperwhites and fragrant ivory roses. "Remember the rule of threes. It was Merrilee last year, now me. You'll be married, too, before you know it."

Brynn had shaken her head and laughed. At thirty, she had no special man in her life, and certainly not one likely to propose. Steady dating, much less marriage, was the furthest thing from her mind. Although she definitely enjoyed men's company— most of her fellow officers were male—she didn't need a man to make her feel complete. She loved her job as a Pleasant Valley police officer and aspired to fill her father's shoes as chief of police someday when he retired. And the people of the valley were her extended family. What woman could want more?

A blast of frigid wind shook the vehicle. Switching on the windshield wipers, she peered through the first flurries of blowing snow, glad she'd donned her department-issue, down-filled parka over her light-weight dress and changed her high-heeled sandals for waterproof boots before she'd left Archer Farm. The early spring snowstorm had timed its arrival just right—after Jodie's wedding and reception had ended, thank goodness.

Reassured by the heavy-duty tires and four-wheel drive of her SUV, Brynn eased onto the highway that led through the valley, filled with small farms, to town. If she drove carefully, she'd have no trouble reaching home before heavy snow, which practically never fell in South Carolina, made the roads impass-able.

To her right in the darkness, the Piedmont River, already swollen with melting winter snows from the surrounding mountains, paralleled the highway. Her car topped a ridge, and, on her left, lights flickered through the trees in front of Grant and Merrilee Na-than's home.

Merrilee, along with Jodie's fifteen-year-old daughter Brittany, had also been bridesmaids at this afternoon's wedding, and Grant and Merrilee had headed home hours ago. Brittany had left soon after to stay with her grandparents for the honeymoon's duration. Brynn had been the last guest to depart.

Valley Road was deserted, and she uttered a prayer of gratitude that the snow was falling so late. By morning, when the locals went about their business, the snowplows would have cleared the accumulated white stuff and made the roads safe and her job easier.

No sooner had those thoughts formed than the blinding glare of headlights filled her rearview mirror. A vehicle was approaching rapidly from behind. Definitely too fast for existing conditions. The speeding car bore down on her, swung into the opposite lane and blasted past, leaving Brynn's SUV vibrating in its vortex.

"Idiot," she muttered under her breath. "He's going to kill himself and someone else if he doesn't slow down."

Keeping her eyes on the road, she reached to the floor of the passenger seat for her portable warning light, popped it onto the dash, and turned on it and her siren. Flooring the accelerator, she took off after the speeder. For now, the falling snow formed only slush on the asphalt, but with temperatures dropping like a rock in a pond, dangerous ice would soon coat the roads, a recipe for disaster.

Brynn grabbed her police radio from the seat beside her and keyed the mike. "This is Officer Sawyer. I'm on Valley Road in pursuit of a silver Jaguar, South Carolina plates." She rattled off the tag number.

"10-4," answered the steady voice of Todd Leland, the night dispatcher. "I'm running the plates now. Do you need backup?"

"10-4." Especially if Todd had a hit on those tags. "Sawyer out." Brynn dropped her radio and gripped the wheel. Ahead, heeding her signals, the Jaguar's driver slowed, pulled to the side of the road, and stopped.

Adrenaline pumping, Brynn parked behind him and switched off her siren. Traffic stops were generally routine, but one going bad was always a possibility. A fleeing felon with nothing to lose wouldn't hesitate to kill a cop to make his escape. She retrieved her off-duty gun from the glove compartment, shoved it into the pocket of her parka and keyed the mike again.

"Anything on those plates yet?"

"It's coming through now, registered to a Randall Benedict on Valley Road. No report of the vehicle being stolen. No outstanding warrants on Benedict. Your backup's on the way."

"10-4." According to Todd's report, the driver was merely stupid, not criminal, but from a cop's point of view, she could never have too much backup. Especially on a deserted road so late at night.

Hiking her long silk skirt above her boots, Brynn slid from the car and used her Maglite to guide her steps to the idling Jaguar. At her approach, the driver's window slid down with an electronic whir.

The driver started to speak. "I have a—"

"I'll do the talking. This is a state highway, not a NASCAR track," Brynn said in the authoritative manner she reserved for lawbreakers, especially those displaying such an obvious lack of common sense. "And the road's icing up. You have a death wish?"

"No." The driver seemed distracted, oblivious to the seriousness of his offense. "I need to—"

"Turn off your engine," Brynn ordered, "and place your hands on the wheel where I can see them."

She shined her flashlight in the driver's face. The man in his midthirties squinted in the brightness, but not before the pupils of his eyes, the color of dark melting chocolate, contracted in the light. She instantly noted the rugged angle of his unshaven jaw, the aristocratic nose, baby-fine brown hair tousled as if he'd just climbed out of bed...

And a wad of one hundred dollar bills thrust under her nose.

Anger burned through her, but she kept a lid on her temper. "If that's a bribe, buster, you're in a heap of trouble."

"No bribe." His tone, although frantic, was rich and full. "Payment for my fine. I can't stop—"

"You can't keep going at your previous speed, either," she said reasonably and struggled to control her fury at the man's arrogance. "You'll kill yourself and someone else—"

"It's Jared. I have to get him to the hospital."

Labored breathing sounded in the back seat. Brynn aimed her light at the source. In a child carrier, a towheaded toddler, damp hair matted to his head and plump cheeks flushed with fever, wheezed violently as his tiny chest struggled for air.

Brynn's anger vanished at the sight of the poor little guy, and her sympathy kicked in. Accustomed to emergencies, she sorted quickly through alternatives. Her four-wheel-drive SUV was safer under present conditions, but removing and reinstalling the child carrier would take time, precious time, judging from the boy's obvious respiratory distress. But the driver—the child's father?—was so rattled, he might wreck his car if left entirely on his own.

"Follow me," Brynn ordered. She'd push her speed, but only as fast as was safe. "I'll radio ahead for the E.R. to expect us. What's Jared's problem?"

"He had a cold, but it's developed into something worse. He's having trouble breathing."

Brynn hurried to her vehicle, drove onto the highway and turned on her siren again. The Jaguar pulled in behind her. After radioing Todd to cancel her backup and alert the hospital, she concentrated on the road, vigilant for signs of ice as she sped through the night, emergency lights flashing.

Questions flitted through her mind. Who was Randall Benedict? She'd never seen the Jaguar's driver before, and she knew everyone who lived on Valley Road. And where was the boy's mother? Wouldn't a kid, especially one as sick as he was, want his mommy?

"Where's Mommy?" four-year-old Brynn asked.

Her mommy had been gone for a long time, and the house was filled with flowers, so many that the overpowering sweetness of their mixed fragrances made her tummy feel sick.

Her father lifted her in his arms. "Mommy's gone to Heaven."

"Wifout me?" Brynn didn't understand, didn't know where Heaven was or why so many people, friends and strangers alike, had gathered at their house, especially without her mother there to greet them. Or why her father's usual big grin had disappeared and he looked so sad.

"Tell her to come home." Frightened, Brynn started to cry. "Right now."

"She can't, pumpkin." Her father looked as if he wanted to cry, too.

"But I want my mommy!" Her wails drew the attention of the people in the room. And then something happened that frightened her as much as her mother's absence. Her big, strong father broke into sobs

and clutched her against his broad chest so tight, it hurt.

Brynn pushed her memories aside to concentrate on the job at hand. She slowed only slightly as Valley Road became Piedmont Avenue, Pleasant Valley's main drag. This late, no stores were open, and the weather was too raw for pedestrians. The Jaguar followed at a safe distance.

After rounding the curve at Jay-Jay's Garage, she pulled into the emergency room entrance of the medical center and parked, grabbed her radio and hurried from the SUV. The Jaguar stopped behind her. Randall Benedict jumped from his car with his boy bundled in his arms and rushed past her.

Trained to form instant assessments, Brynn noted that the man was tall, well over six feet, but with an athletic build, apparent even under his expensive camel-colored cashmere overcoat. Beneath it, she caught a glimpse of designer sweatpants and an immaculate T-shirt. Judging from his Gucci loafers without socks, he'd dressed in a hurry. Even in his disheveled state, the man looked too handsome to be true. Had to be fantastically good-looking, Brynn admitted, for her to notice. Too bad he was married. And where was his wife, anyway? What woman in her right mind wouldn't want to spend every minute with such a gorgeous husband and adorable little boy? What mother wouldn't stay with her seriously ill child?

Possibilities flitted through Brynn's mind. Benedict could be divorced, but that seemed unlikely. Only under the most unusual circumstances did judges take a child as young as Jared from his mother. More feasible was the probability that Mrs. Benedict simply hadn't arrived in Pleasant Valley yet. The man was a newcomer. Perhaps his wife had remained at their former home to oversee its sale and the loading of moving vans. Or she could be on a business trip. Or taking care of a sick parent. Any number of reasons could explain her absence.

Brynn studied Randall Benedict closer. After her first glimpse of him, he appeared remarkably self-confident and self-possessed. He moved and spoke with the ease of a man who knew what he wanted and was accustomed to getting it. Further inspection revealed worried furrows in his high forehead, the edge of tension around his generous mouth and a slight tick below his right eye at his sculpted cheekbone. Although his entire body was rigid with anxiety, he cradled the toddler with remarkable tenderness.

"Hang on, tiger," he murmured in a reassuring tone. "The doctor's going to help you feel better."

"Wanna go home," the boy wheezed.

"We'll go home soon," Benedict promised with a gentleness at odds with his earlier response to Brynn. He paused as she caught up with them. "I can't thank you enough for your help," he said to her.

"No problem. That's my job. Let's get your son inside."

"He's not—" Benedict began, but stopped, shook his head and hurried toward the entrance.

Not going to make it. She shoved the pessimistic thought aside. "Jared will be fine. Dr. Anderson's a very competent physician."

Brynn accompanied them through the automatic doors of the emergency room, where Dr. Scott Anderson, the young E.R. specialist who'd joined the hospital staff last year, was waiting for them in the foyer. The doctor motioned Benedict and Jared into a treatment room, followed with a nurse in tow and closed the door. Brynn took a deep breath and exhaled slowly. She hadn't realized how tense she'd been until relief washed over her that the little boy was now in the doctor's capable hands.

While she waited for news of Jared's condition, Brynn stopped at the desk to speak with Emily Carmichael, one of the night nurses. As Emily chattered away, Brynn couldn't stop thinking about Randall Benedict, who stirred her interest. And so attractive he'd stirred her senses in a way no other man ever had. Just her luck to find the one man she might like to know better was almost certainly married and with a son. She considered family sacred, which made Benedict definitely off-limits and reinforced her conviction that she was meant for single life. Catching Jodie's bouquet had been a fluke that had sent Brynn's thoughts in directions they had no business taking. As far as marriage was concerned, she was wedded to her job. Period. End of story.

"Looks like you just came from Jodie's wedding." Emily pointed to Brynn's long skirt with a hint of wistfulness. "We were all invited, but some of us had to work. I drew the short straw."

"Get used to it, Em," Brynn said with a sympathetic smile. She'd had to pull a few strings and juggle duty rosters to attend her best friend's nuptials. "Duty comes first in our lines of work."

The young nurse, only months out of college, nodded. "Want some coffee?"

Brynn checked the clock on the wall behind the desk. She wouldn't leave until she'd had a report on Jared and could be in for a long night. "Sure. High-octane with cream and sugar, please."

Emily disappeared into the break room and returned moments later with two foam cups. She handed one to Brynn and nodded toward the treatment room. "Must be tough, having a sick kid."

Brynn sipped her coffee and attempted to put a lid on her worry over the little boy. So small and vulnerable, he'd touched her heart and broken through the objectivity she worked so hard to maintain on the job. "Illness is a fact of life."

Emily cocked her head and considered Brynn through narrowed eyes. "You've been a cop how long?"

"Eight years."

"That explains it."

"What?"

"Why you're so cynical."

"Sheesh, Em, don't spare my feelings," Brynn said with pretended hurt. "Just spit out what you really think."

"We've spent a lot of time together since I started work here," Emily began.

Brynn nodded. Too much time. She'd logged more hours in the E.R. than she cared to remember, interviewing victims of accidents, domestic abuse and the rare but disturbing casualties of assault and other crimes. "And your point is?"

Emily shrugged. "You act like none of this—" her gesture encompassed the E.R. "—touches you."

Brynn blinked in surprise. Did she really come across so hard-boiled? "If you don't maintain emotional distance, jobs like ours will burn you out fast."

"That's easier said than done." Emily admitted with a sigh. "Especially when kids like that sweet little boy are concerned, bless his heart."

Brynn had to agree. Worrying about Jared had shaken her more than she cared to admit. "A sense of humor helps."

"Any new jokes?" Emily asked.

Brynn grinned, happy to change the subject. "How can you tell if it's a skunk or a lawyer who's been run over on the highway?"

"I give up."

"There're skid marks around the skunk." Emily's laugh encouraged Brynn to continue. "How many lawyers does it take to change a lightbulb?"

"How many?"

"How many can you afford?"

Emily chuckled again and shook her head. "You know more lawyer jokes than anyone I've ever met. Do you really dislike them so much?"

"Lawyers? I like 'em about as much as I like Yankees," Brynn admitted.

"I always figured lawyers and the police are on the same side."

Brynn snorted with disgust. "If I had ten bucks for every criminal who's lawyered up and gotten off scot-free because some crooked attorney manipulated the system, I could buy a luxury condo at Myrtle Beach."

Emily folded her arms on the admissions desk. "But not all lawyers are crooked."

"No," Brynn admitted with a straight face. "Some are dead."

"You are so bad," Emily laughed and shook her head.

Although Brynn had made her comments in jest, she recognized her prejudice. For the most part, she considered herself fair and open-minded, but attorneys and Northerners pushed her buttons. Where attorneys were concerned, she agreed with the principle that every person was entitled to the best defense possible, but the shady shenanigans of too many unprincipled lawyers had left a bad taste in her mouth for the profession as a whole.

And she hoped Emily wouldn't get her started on Yankees. They flooded the town every summer, in their big RVs and fancy cars, passing through on their way to summer homes in the nearby mountains. Not that she envied their wealth. They'd probably worked hard for it. What Brynn disliked was their condescension, treating the locals like dim-witted morons from *The Beverly Hillbillies,* laughing at Southern drawls and taking great pleasure in explaining how much better everything was done up North.

Two particular Yankees had caused plenty of trouble recently in Pleasant Valley. Ginger Parker, with the morals of an alley cat in heat, had almost ruined Jim and Cat Stratton's marriage. Ginger had been from New Jersey. And the antiques dealer who'd tried to rip off sweet old Mrs. Weatherstone had been based in Rhode Island.

Not that there weren't Southern snakes in abundance, but, at least in a five-county radius, Brynn knew who they were. Strangers, especially from the North, always put her on alert and on edge. If that attitude made her opinionated, it also made her cautious. And she couldn't be too cautious in her line of work.

"You don't fool me," Emily was saying. "I know

you too well. For all your ranting about lawyers and Yankees, you'd be first on the scene if either needed help. And you'd provide it gladly."

"That's my job," Brynn countered.

Before she could say more, Dr. Anderson came out of the treatment room and approached the desk.

"How's the kid?" Brynn asked.

The young doctor pursed his lips, then sighed. "He's in severe respiratory distress. I have him on oxygen and antibiotics. We'll have to wait and see how well he can fight this off."

Brynn's heart went out to the little boy, so ill without his mother. "How soon before he's out of the woods?"

"Depends on how strong he is. Could be a couple of hours. Could be a few days." The doctor's solemn expression indicated a third possibility. The boy might not recover at all.

Brynn felt a rush of sympathy, not only for Jared, but for his father. She couldn't imagine how Randall Benedict was feeling now, without anyone to stand watch with him over his sick child.

Her radio squawked and she keyed the mike. "Sawyer here."

"We have an accident with injuries west of Carsons Corner," the dispatcher announced. "I've dispatched Rhodes."

"Understood," Brynn replied. "I'm coming in."

The Pleasant Valley police department was small,

usually manned at night by only the dispatcher and one patrol officer. In bad weather or other emergencies, additional help was needed, and Brynn often had to pull an extra shift. With the police station across the street from the medical center and a clean uniform in her locker, she could report for duty in mere minutes.

Brynn said goodbye to Dr. Anderson and Emily and headed for her car. But she couldn't get Randall Benedict and Jared, a worried parent alone in a strange town and his dangerously ill little boy, out of her mind. She turned before exiting the automatic doors.

"I'll drop by later to see how the kid's doing," she said before plunging into the night and the blowing snow.

Chapter Two

The light pressure of a hand on his shoulder jolted
Rand out of a deep sleep. He came instantly awake
and centered his attention immediately on Jared.
The boy, dwarfed by the hospital bed, lay still.

Too still.

Terror squeezed Rand's lungs like a fist, and he
couldn't move from the hard plastic chair where
he'd slept. Couldn't breathe. "My God, he's not—"

"Jared's fine," a drawling feminine voice assured
him. "The crisis has passed. His fever's broken, and
he's breathing without difficulty now."

Relief cascaded through him, and, for the first
time, Rand became aware of the woman whose hand
still grasped his shoulder. "You're sure?"

"Dr. Anderson was just in, but he didn't wake
you. You've had a long night."

Sunlight filtered through the curtains of the
hospital window, and Rand checked his watch—
8:00 a.m.

He stood, leaned over Jared, and placed his hand on the boy's forehead. The toddler's color was normal, his fever gone, his breathing easier. The oxygen mask had been removed. Weak with relief, Rand turned to the nurse—

And saw instead the police officer who'd escorted him into town.

"You here to arrest me?" His mind, fuzzy from lack of sleep, struggled to make sense of the officer's presence.

His question apparently took her by surprise. "Arrest you?"

"For speeding. I know I was driving like a bat out of hell last night, but—"

"I just stopped by to check on Jared."

She smiled, and suddenly she was no longer an officer but the most beautiful woman Rand had ever seen. Midnight-blue eyes glowed with compassion, and her mouth turned up at the corners in an alluring smile. Even with her auburn hair tucked neatly into a French braid, it appeared thick and luxurious, the kind of hair he'd love to run his fingers through. And its color complemented perfectly the apricot flush of her cheeks and her flawless complexion. Tall—she had to be at least five foot eight—her body filled her navy blue uniform so sensually it should have been against the law. In contrast to the severe lines of her uniform, the faintest hint of her floral scent swirled through the room.

When he'd rushed Jared into the E.R. last night, Rand had been so frantic with worry that the police officer's appearance had barely registered. Otherwise, he would have noted those spectacular eyes, like the blue velvet of a moonless summer sky. Even if he hadn't been distracted, he couldn't have seen how curvaceous she was. She'd been bundled up in her police parka and a long dress. Long dress? Had she really been wearing one or had his worry-crazed mind played tricks on him?

"You okay?" she asked.

He flushed, embarrassed that he'd been staring. "What?"

"You've had a rough night. You should go home and get some sleep." Her words, slow and sensual, made him think of the heady fragrance of magnolias and steamy Southern nights.

"I won't leave Jared alone." He checked once more to reassure himself that Jared was truly better.

"Anyone I can notify for you?" she asked.

He shook his head. "Thanks—" His gaze traveled to the name tag on the pocket above the enticing curve of her breast. "Officer Sawyer—"

"Call me Brynn." She offered her hand.

He grasped it and noted instantly the contrast of cool, silky skin, long elegant fingers and a no-nonsense grip that he released with reluctance. "Thanks, Brynn, but I have my cell phone if I need it. And I'm Rand, by the way."

"I can stay while you take a break. I don't mind. He's a sweet little kid."

"You're very kind, but, no. Jared's had a tough time lately, and when he wakes up, he should see a familiar face."

"At least let me bring you breakfast."

He scrutinized her closely, assessing her motives. She wasn't coming on to him. In spite of her obvious sexual attributes, she didn't flaunt them. Her concern seemed genuine with no strings attached, probably an example of the legendary Southern hospitality he'd heard so much about.

"Doesn't the hospital have a cafeteria?" he asked.

"You can eat here if you're a masochist," she replied with a friendly grin. "But Jodie's Café is just down the street. They have the best cranberry-pecan muffins in the Upstate."

"Upstate?"

"Northwest South Carolina."

"Sorry. I haven't learned the local lingo."

"You live on Valley Road, right?"

"Just moved in. I bought the place called River Walk."

Her magnificent eyes widened at his mention of the name. "Great location, right on the river. Good trout fishing."

"And lots of fresh air and sunshine. Just what the doctor ordered for Jared's health." He glanced at

Jared, sleeping peacefully, and felt a stab of guilt. "Guess I didn't get him out of New York fast enough."

"You're from New York?" Brynn's question seemed strained.

"New York City. Jared and I moved to River Walk to escape the pollution. Jared, as you can tell, has weak lungs. I'm hoping the country air will improve his stamina."

Brynn flashed a brittle smile. "Will you be working in town?"

He shook his head. "I'm with a New York law firm."

A wary look flashed across her very pretty face. "You're a lawyer?"

Rand frowned. She'd uttered the word in a derogatory tone usually reserved for wife beaters, serial killers and child pornographers. "A corporate attorney."

She backed toward the door. "Not many corporations in Pleasant Valley."

"I'm taking a sabbatical, time for us to settle into our new life."

Brynn reached behind her and grabbed the doorknob. "Dr. Anderson says Jared should recover completely in a day or two. That new antibiotic did the trick."

Rand didn't want her to leave. Not until he'd learned a whole lot more about the delectable Officer Sawyer. "Come to dinner when Jared's better. I'd like to show you our place."

Now *that* was the understatement of the year.

"Maybe." Brynn couldn't have sounded more non-committal. "I'll have the café send that breakfast over."

Before Rand could protest, she slipped out the door and closed it firmly behind her. Officer Sawyer hadn't appeared the type who would spook easily. He sank back into the bedside chair, wondering what he'd said that had sent her running as if the devil were at her heels.

BRYNN STOMPED through the snow that covered the sidewalk, heedless of the creeping dampness at the cuffs of her uniform trousers, oblivious to the cold that nipped her cheeks. As steamed as she felt, she was amazed the snow didn't melt in her path. How could she be so stupid, going all fluttery inside over a guy with three strikes against him?

Married, most likely. He hadn't been wearing a wedding band, but that wasn't concrete proof of anything.

Yankee, by his own admission.

And a lawyer.

But try as she might, she couldn't get Rand Benedict out of her mind, especially the way his deep brown eyes had widened first with surprise, then blatant approval when she'd seen him this morning. And that voice. No nasal Yankee twang. Just seductively rich, deep and smooth, like an anchorman's on the network news.

He had shed his cashmere overcoat, too, using it as a blanket over his knees, exposing broad shoulders, well-developed biceps and an enticing chest beneath his pristine white T-shirt. Sitting at a desk and hoisting law books didn't produce that kind of physical perfection. He probably worked out in an expensive Fifth Avenue health club. In New York City, for Pete's sake! She'd have more in common with the man if he came from Mars.

Then why couldn't she get him out of her head? He'd occupied her thoughts during the entire night shift, causing Todd Leland to eye her more than once with curiosity when he had to repeat a question. Fortunately, she hadn't been called out on the road. In her present state of out-of-her-mind, she'd have ended up with Jay-Jay pulling her patrol car from a snowbank with his tow truck.

Brynn had worried all night about little Jared, too. She could have simply called the hospital to check on him once her shift was over. But, no, she'd gone and stuck herself smack-dab in temptation's path by returning to the hospital where Rand Benedict would be waiting.

Reaching the entrance to Jodie's Mountain Crafts and Café, Brynn stomped the snow off her boots and opened one of the double glass doors. A blast of warm air and a mélange of delicious aromas greeted her. In a couple months, the café would be crowded with tourists stopping for breakfast on their way to the North Carolina mountains, but in late March, the working locals had already eaten and left, and the dining area was practically empty.

"Morning, Officer Sawyer."

Sixteen-year-old Daniel, a teen from Archer Farm whom Jodie had hired as a busboy, looked up from the table he was clearing. Of all Jeff's clients, Daniel had made the most progress in rehabilitating himself. Tall and lanky with carrot-colored hair and freckles, Daniel had gained poise and self-confidence over the past few months. And a reputation as a hard worker.

"Hey, Daniel," Brynn greeted him. "Do you have time to make a delivery for me?"

His face lighted with its usual puppy-dog eagerness. "Yes, ma'am!"

"Take a large coffee, large o.j. and several kinds of muffins over to the hospital. To Mr. Rand Benedict. And put them on my tab."

"Yes, ma'am." Daniel tucked the tub of dirty dishes under his arm and hurried toward the kitchen.

Just because Rand was off-limits didn't mean he didn't deserve a little pampering after the hard night he'd endured. She'd promised him breakfast, and with that obligation fulfilled, she'd forget him.

Brynn wandered through the gift area, a wide hall lined with shelves filled with handmade quilts, willow baskets and rustic birdhouses, many made by the boys at Archer Farm. The passage led to the dining room on the deck overlooking the river. The arching glass roof and walls kept out the snow and cold and provided a breathtaking view of the Piedmont River below and the mountains beyond.

"Hey, honeybun, come sit with us," a familiar voice called.

Brynn's aunt, Marion Sawyer, sat with Merrilee Nathan at the only occupied table on the deck. Glad for an excuse not to be alone with her troublesome thoughts, Brynn joined them.

"You two are up early," Brynn said.

"I'm filling in as hostess for the breakfast shift while Jodie's on her honeymoon," Merrilee explained. Her face flushed and her eyes glimmered at the mention of the honeymoon, and Brynn guessed Merrilee was recalling her own last summer with her veterinarian husband Grant, who was Jodie's brother.

"And I have a house to show at nine o'clock," Aunt Marion explained, "although the clients may cancel because of the weather."

Brynn shrugged off her parka and took a seat at the table. Merrilee retrieved a mug and silverware from a nearby serving station and poured Brynn's coffee.

"You didn't sell River Walk, by any chance?" Brynn asked Marion. Along with her husband, Bud, Marion ran the local real estate office.

"Don't I wish?" the older woman with huge bones, big hair, a strong jaw and a heart as large as the rest of her said. "That commission alone would have equaled my last year's income."

Brynn had never been inside the riverside "cabin," a massive log home with expansive windows and multitiered decks, built before she was born, but she'd often checked out the exterior of the empty house while on patrol. "Isn't it in pretty rough shape?"

"Needs some cosmetic repairs," Marion agreed, "new appliances and upgrades in the bathrooms, but it's still a valuable property with over five thousand square feet, a guest house and location, location, location."

"How come you're so interested in River Walk?" Merrilee leaned forward and eyed Brynn closely, like a bloodhound scenting a trail.

"Aren't you?" Brynn sidestepped the question. "It's practically across the highway from you and Grant."

"And it's sold?" Merrilee asked.

"Apparently." Brynn filled them in on her encounter with Rand and Jared Benedict.

"Poor little kid," Marion murmured. "Dr. Anderson's sure he's going to be all right?"

Brynn nodded, sipped her coffee and tried to ignore the laserlike glare of Merrilee's sky-blue gaze.

"What aren't you telling us?" Merrilee asked.

"About what?"

"About Rand Benedict." Merrilee exchanged a long look with Marion.

"I've told you everything I know about the man," Brynn insisted with a shrug, striving for nonchalance.

Merrilee narrowed her eyes. "You haven't told

us why you're absolutely glowing when you talk about him."

"I'm glowing because I just walked two blocks in the snow, *not* because he asked me to dinner." Brynn started to push away from the table, but Marion grabbed her wrist.

"Whoa, not so fast," her aunt said.

Cornered, Brynn sank into her chair. "What?"

"Tell us the rest," Marion said.

"I told you—"

"—the bare bones," Merrilee interrupted. "Now fill in the blanks."

Irritated at their persistence, Brynn ran a finger under the suddenly too-tight collar of her uniform. "There are no blanks."

Merrilee shook her head. "This is Merrilee June, your old buddy, you're talking to, your friend who's taken part in every bit of mischief you've ever committed. I know that look, Brynn."

"The dead-tired-after-working-all-night-and-want-to-go-home-and-sleep look?" Brynn hedged.

"Un-uh." Merrilee shook her head. "The I'm-hiding-something look."

"What would I have to hide?" Brynn asked, feigning innocence.

"That's what we're trying to find out," Aunt Marion said. "What's this Rand Benedict look like?"

Handsome as sin. Good enough to eat. Pulse-pounding perfect. "He's nice looking."

Merrilee rolled her eyes. "C'mon, Brynn. I can tell you're interested in the guy. You get this soft, misty look when you talk about him."

"I am *not* interested. And even if I were, he's a married Yankee lawyer." She didn't know for certain he was married, but claiming the fact would help get her off the hook. She hoped.

"You sure he's married?" Marion asked. Brynn's aunt had been trying to find a husband for her only niece since Brynn had turned eighteen. Having gone through all the eligible bachelors in Pleasant Valley and the surrounding counties, Marion obviously viewed Rand Benedict as fresh meat.

"He has a son," Brynn said, hoping to convince them that Benedict was unavailable. "He's bought a house too huge for just the two of them. Maybe he's waiting for his wife to join him."

"Maybe he's divorced," Merrilee countered.

"Well, hot damn," Brynn said with more sarcasm than she'd intended. "That would make him a real catch. A *divorced* Yankee lawyer."

"Maybe the two of you could find something in common," Aunt Marion, ever the optimist, suggested.

"Maybe the two of you should mind your own business," Brynn said with a smile to soften her words. "I'm not in the market for a man."

"Then there's no reason why you shouldn't accept his dinner offer," Marion responded with maddening logic.

"And every reason why you should," Merrilee added.

"Name one," Brynn shot back, outflanked and outnumbered.

"He's new in town." Merrilee studied her perfect pink fingernails with exasperating calm. "You should make him feel welcome."

Aunt Marion bent her head toward Brynn, her eyes flashing with curiosity. "And you'd have the perfect opportunity to learn more about him."

"Why would I want to know?" Brynn refused to admit how much the prospect of discovering more about Rand appealed to her.

"Pffft," Marion snorted. "This is Pleasant Valley, honeybun. Everyone wants to know everything about everyone else. And it's particularly important for the police to have all the facts. Think how much trouble Jim and Cat Stratton might have avoided if you had dug up the goods on that Ginger Parker when she first came to town."

"I'm a police officer," Brynn said. "If you want someone to dig up dirt on Rand Benedict, hire a private eye."

"We're not suggesting the man has skeletons in his closet," Merrilee said with a shake of her pretty blond curls. "If he really is a single parent with a small son, he needs the help of a supportive community."

"From what I saw," Brynn said, "Rand Benedict can afford to pay for all the help he needs."

"You can't buy friends," Merrilee observed quietly.

Brynn winced. Maybe police work had made her cynical, just as Emily had said. "You're right," she conceded with a sigh. "If the man asks me again, I'll consider going to dinner."

Hope flared in Marion's eyes, and Brynn was quick to add, "But just because it's the neighborly thing to do, and I only said I'd *consider* it. By the way, what did you think of Jodie and Jeff's cutting their wedding cake with a Marine officer's saber yesterday? That's a first for Pleasant Valley."

With the subject safely shifted, Brynn leaned back in her chair and enjoyed her coffee. Rand Benedict lived out of town and didn't seem the type to mix with the locals. In a few days, Aunt Marion, Merrilee and Brynn herself, she hoped, would forget all about him. After all, the man had said he was on sabbatical, not a permanent resident. She'd probably never see him again.

Over a week later, Brynn surveyed the eager young faces of Mrs. Shepherd's third-grade class with a sentimental sense of déjà vu. It didn't seem that long ago that she and Jodie had sat next to each other in the rows beside the windows and Merrilee had been in the first grade classroom down the hall.

Outside the tall windows of the ancient brick building, a row of spectacular Bradford pear trees bloomed like stalks of white cotton candy against the brilliant blue sky. Beneath them, beds of cheerful yellow daffodils, hearty survivors of the brief spring storm, nodded in the breeze. Last week's snow had melted almost immediately, replaced by warm balmy days that had induced an outbreak of spring fever in the school's population. Needing a diversion from routine, Mrs. Shepherd had asked Brynn to present her Officer Friendly program to the class.

Brynn had completed her standard talk on avoiding strangers and observing traffic and gun-safety rules and was handing out junior officer cards when she noted a newcomer who had just slipped in the rear door and joined the parent volunteers at the back of the class.

Rand Benedict.

What was he doing at the elementary school? Jared wasn't old enough to enroll. But Rand, dressed with great casual style in khaki chinos and a sage-green knit shirt that brought out the deep brown of his eyes, sat with one hip propped atop a low bookcase, perfectly at ease, as if he had every right to be there.

He'd phoned the station several times over the past week and left Brynn messages, asking her to return his calls, but she hadn't. In spite of her halfway promise to Merrilee and Marion, she didn't intend to accept his dinner invitation. Being alone with a man she found both entirely too appealing and at the same time completely wrong for her would be an exercise in frustration. By not responding to his calls, Brynn had hoped to make him realize she wasn't interested. And until this moment, she'd believed her lack of response had worked.

"Now, class," Mrs. Shepherd was saying, "before Officer Sawyer leaves, does anyone have questions?"

Brynn dragged her attention from Rand to the class. In the front row, Kenny Fulton, a skinny little hellion whose father owned the town's only department store, waved his hand. "Have you ever shot anybody?"

Aware of Rand's gaze, which was making her cheeks flush and her body temperature rise, Brynn answered, "No, Kenny, fortunately, I've never had to draw my gun in the line of duty."

"How come?" the boy demanded.

"Because most people have enough respect for the law to do what an officer says without the need to display deadly force."

Kenny screwed his face in disgust. "What's the fun of having a gun if you can't shoot it."

The class laughed, and Brynn smiled. "Oh, I shoot it a lot. At target practice. Anyone who carries a gun must know how and when to use it."

"Officer Sawyer is being modest," Mrs. Shepherd interrupted. "She has a caseful of trophies that she's won in shooting competitions all over the country."

"Awesome," Jennifer Clayton, a redhead in the middle of the room, who reminded Brynn of herself at that age, said. "Just like Annie Oakley. We learned about her this year."

Sid Paulie, whose folks ran the drugstore, stuck his hand in the air as if grasping for a lifeline.

"Yes, Sid?" Mrs. Shepherd said.

The boy sat up straight, pleased to be recognized. "How much money do you make, Officer Sawyer?"

In the back of the room, Rand shifted his weight and crossed his arms over his broad chest. Interest sparked in his expression, and Brynn felt a smidgeon of irritation. The clothes he wore today probably cost more than her pay for the month, so why was he so captivated by her finances?

But her salary always came up in school sessions, so she had her stock answer ready, thank goodness, because Rand's steady scrutiny was turning her brain to mush.

"Police officers make about the same as schoolteachers," Brynn explained to Sid. "It's not a lot of money, but enough for a decent living. People who become police officers and teachers don't choose those jobs for the money. They do them because they like to help people."

Kenny raised his hand again. "How do the police help people? Don't you just give them tickets or lock them in jail?"

Brynn opened her mouth to answer, but a voice at the back of the room beat her to a response.

"May I answer that, Mrs. Shepherd?"

Looking more flustered than Brynn had ever seen her, the veteran teacher peered at Rand, apparently noting his presence in the midst of the other adult volunteers for the first time. "And you are?"

"Rand Benedict." He held up the laminated visitor card on a lanyard around his neck to indicate he'd checked in with the office. "I recently moved to Pleasant Valley. Last week during the snowstorm, my boy Jared was dangerously ill and having trouble breathing. I was rushing him to the hospital when Officer Sawyer came along, radioed ahead to the emergency room and led the way to the hospital with lights flashing and sirens wailing. That's one example of how the police help people," he explained to the class.

"Is Jared okay?" Jennifer asked.

"He's fine now, thanks to Officer Sawyer and Dr. Anderson." Rand seemed as at ease among the children and parents as if he spoke to strangers every day. That confidence, Brynn thought, must give him a hell of a courtroom presence.

Jimmy Clayton, Jennifer's twin brother, spoke up. "There was an accident on the highway near our farm last year. Officer Sawyer gave the driver CPR until the ambulance got there. My dad said she probably saved the lady's life."

"So you see, Kenny," Mrs. Shepherd explained

with a kindly smile, "police officers do much more than give tickets and lock people up."

"Thank you, class," Brynn said, anxious to make her escape. "You've been an excellent audience."

She turned to leave, but Rand spoke again from the back of the room. "Mrs. Shepherd, may I ask one more question?"

Irritated by his interruptions and struggling not to show her annoyance, Brynn turned back toward the class.

"Of course, Mr. Benedict," Mrs. Shepherd answered with her characteristic courtesy.

Rand nodded and locked gazes with Brynn, who felt skewered like a butterfly on a pin with no hope of escape. She forced herself to relax. Just one more question and she was out of here. And away from the magnetic charm of Rand Benedict.

"Officer Sawyer." Rand addressed her directly, and even from the back of the room, she could read the devil in his eyes. "May I speak with you outside?"

Chapter Three

The children in the classroom turned and stared at Rand with open curiosity. Mrs. Shepherd smiled as if she'd just guessed an interesting secret. The adult volunteers on either side of him exchanged knowing looks. Only Brynn didn't react, but stood at the front of the room as if carved from stone, her posture rigid, her expression impassive. She didn't give him a clue to what she was thinking.

Suddenly his bright idea of confronting her publicly didn't seem so bright after all.

He moved quickly toward the rear door of the class, but Brynn became instantly animated and made a swift but dignified exit through the door at the front of the room. She had a lead on him as she hurried through the hall to the exit, so he ran to catch up with her.

This might be his only chance, and he didn't want to blow it. He'd been trying for a week to contact her, and pulling this stunt showed how desperate he'd become.

He couldn't help it. Ever since the night of Jared's illness, she'd haunted his thoughts. God knew what would have happened to him and Jared if she hadn't miraculously appeared. Rand knew nothing about children. He knew even less about sick children. When Jared's breathing difficulty had begun, Rand had panicked, shoved Jared into the car and taken off in the direction of town in search of a hospital. When Brynn's siren sounded behind him, he'd been horrified to discover he was traveling ninety-five miles an hour on a dark, unfamiliar road. If she hadn't pulled him over, he might have killed himself and Jared. He'd been so rattled, he'd been barely coherent when she'd stood by his car window and read him the riot act. As soon as he'd gathered his wits enough to inform her of Jared's illness, she'd transformed into an angel in navy blue. As he'd watched over his sleeping child during the days and nights of Jared's recovery, Brynn had filled his thoughts.

And gratitude wasn't all he felt. In his corporate career, he'd met plenty of slick, sophisticated, smart women, elegantly attired, carefully coiffed, magnificently made-up. But he'd never encountered a woman with Brynn's genuinely natural beauty—and a warm heart to match. Fate had thrown so much sorrow his way recently, Rand considered meeting Brynn compensation for the sadness in his life, and he wasn't about to let her get away.

"Brynn, wait!"

She barreled through the double exit doors into the sunshine, then wheeled to face him, fists on her hips, her eyes blazing with annoyance. "You have some nerve!"

The deep blue hue of her eyes matched her uniform, and the sunlight sparked golden highlights in her auburn hair. Her full lips pursed in disapproval, her strong but lovely chin jutted at a defiant angle, and a delicate vein pulsed in the slender column of her throat.

"I was desperate," he said.

"Desperate for what?" she demanded. "To embarrass the living daylights out of me? Everyone in town will hear about this and jump to all the wrong conclusions."

I was desperate to convince myself you're as magnificent as I remembered, he thought. *To persuade you to know me better.*

"To get in touch with you." He couldn't believe how calm he sounded when his heart was racing, not only from his sprint down the hall but from the sight of her in all her outraged glory. "You didn't return my calls."

"I've been busy." This time she avoided his gaze, and he knew she lied.

"You have to eat," he said.

"What?"

"All I ask is that you have dinner with me, to let me thank you for your help the night of Jared's illness."

"You've thanked me already. Dinner isn't necessary." She pivoted on one foot and headed toward the parking lot.

He fell in step beside her. "Are you always this rude?"

She stopped again and turned on him. "Me? Rude? You're the one who interrupted Mrs. Shepherd's class."

"I didn't interrupt. In fact, I contributed to the discussion."

"With a request to speak privately with me?"

"How else was I supposed to get in touch with you, when you won't return my calls?"

"Did it ever occur to you I have good reason not to return your calls?"

"Name one."

"You're married."

"I'm not."

She stopped suddenly. "Divorced, then."

"Not guilty."

Her features spasmed with regret. "You're a widower?"

He shook his head.

Puzzlement replaced regret on her lovely face. "But you have a son."

"Jared's not my son."

Her eyes narrowed. "Then why is he with you?"

"I promise you, I haven't kidnapped him."

He could almost see the wheels turning in her mind. He'd thrown her a puzzle, one her investigative curiosity couldn't resist. He wasn't at liberty to divulge everything and would have to be careful not to reveal his true motives for coming to Pleasant Valley. If they became known, they could spoil his chances for success.

"Come to my place for dinner tonight, and I'll explain everything." *Well, almost everything.* "Lillian, by the way, has finally arrived and is an excellent cook, so you'll be well fed."

"Who's Lillian?"

"Eight o'clock?" he persisted.

She folded her arms across her chest, drawing his attention to the sweet curves that even the severe cut of her uniform couldn't hide, and leaned her head to one side, as if considering.

"If I accept your invitation, will you leave me alone?"

Her request shocked him. "I'm not a stalker."

"Then how did you know where I was?"

He jerked his thumb behind him to the building across the street. "I stopped by the police station, hoping to run into you. The dispatcher told me I'd find you here."

"If I have dinner with you, will you leave me alone?" she repeated.

"Brynn, I just want to show my thanks—"

She cocked one eyebrow in clear disbelief.

"Okay," he admitted. As a police officer, she probably had a built-in B.S. detector, so he settled on honesty. "I'd also like to have you as a friend. I don't know anyone in town, and since I'm going to be here awhile…"

Honesty apparently was the best policy. Her expression softened and the fire in her eyes cooled. "I suppose one dinner wouldn't hurt."

He relied on his courtroom face to keep his elation from showing. "Dress casually and warm. It's cold on the river at night."

"Eight o'clock tonight," she said with a nod and walked away.

And didn't look back.

BRYNN PULLED a pair of wool slacks from her closet, held them against her in front of the mirror, then tossed them in exasperation on the growing pile on her bed. Casual dress, Rand had said, but somehow her usual jeans and sweatshirt didn't seem appropriate for dinner at River Walk.

Why had she accepted his invitation in the first place, she wondered with self-disgust.

Curiosity, her image in the mirror answered. *You're dying to know why your initial assumptions were off base. Rand Benedict is neither married nor divorced, and Jared isn't his son. You want to know the real scoop.*

"Why should I care?" Brynn dragged a long denim skirt from the closet.

He's a mystery. And if there's one thing you can't resist, it's a mystery.

"Okay." She was talking to the mirror again, a sure sign she was losing her mind. "I can't stand a mystery, but I can definitely resist *him*. He's still a Yankee lawyer."

A delectably handsome Yankee lawyer with a smile that makes your knees wobble. And he's deliciously tall. You're five-eight and he towers over you—

"Oh, shut up," she snapped at her reflection.

She yanked a white turtleneck, an embroidered denim vest and black Italian boots from the closet, added them to the long denim skirt, and dressed hurriedly. Her selection would have to do. She was just going for dinner, for Pete's sake, not an audience with the queen.

Because her friends and family would pester her to death for details and jump to all the wrong conclusions, she hadn't told anyone she'd accepted Rand's invitation. Except Todd Leland, the dispatcher. And she'd fibbed to him a little, saying she was just going out to River Walk to check on Jared. Between her off-duty gun and her skills at hand-to-hand fighting, she wasn't concerned about her safety, but having her whereabouts known was always a wise precaution, in case of emergencies.

Half an hour later, she turned her SUV off Valley Road onto the long drive that curved through banks of deep glossy green rhododendron. At the final bend of the road, River Walk shone through the darkness in all its glory. Built in the late sixties as a summer getaway for an Atlanta millionaire, the magnificent log mansion stood three stories high on a bluff above the river. Walls of glass extended to the peaks and gables of the undulating roofline, and welcoming light streamed through the panes onto the surrounding decks, a series of tiers that descended to the river, with the final level extending over the rushing waters below.

Vacant for decades, the expensive property had been an occasional seasonal rental until placed on the market last year. And Rand Benedict had been the lucky buyer. The man had to have more money than God to afford such a place, just one more area where she and the attorney had absolutely nothing in common.

Then why was she here, she asked herself for the one hundredth time.

Pure, unadulterated nosiness, the fatal kind that dooms curious felines.

Parking on the wide flagstone landing beside the front steps, she hoped the answers she found tonight would quell her runaway curiosity. Just thinking about Rand stirred too many unfamiliar feelings she didn't want to deal with, emotions she'd previously been able to sublimate in the cool objectivity that her job required—

Until she'd met Rand Benedict, who'd rattled her calm detachment as no one else had done before. And she couldn't figure why. She was used to handsome men. She'd been surrounded her entire life by alpha males, police officers and farmers, big strapping men who lived with gusto and commanded respect, yet none had left her breathless, sped her pulse or quickened her interest as this Yankee stranger had.

Inhaling a deep breath of the chilly night air to steady herself, she gathered the Officer Friendly teddy bear, her purse and a heavy wool shawl from the passenger seat, stepped from the car and climbed the stairs toward the front entry.

The massive carved wooden door swung open before she reached it, and Rand stood in a pool of light with Jared in his arms. How did the man manage to look more attractive every time she saw him? Tonight he could have passed for a cover model for *GQ* in tight designer jeans, a bulky beige fisherman's sweater and tooled leather boots. And beneath that handsome facade, she suspected, were rock-hard strength and a brilliant mind.

Jared, arms tight around Rand's neck, hid his face against Rand's shoulder.

"Welcome to River Walk," Rand said.

Brynn stepped inside, and the magnificent architecture drew her attention from her host.

"Wow." Brynn winced inwardly at her automatic naive response to the house's interior. If Rand didn't already consider her a typical hayseed, she'd just given him cause.

The wide foyer with its soaring timber-framed

ceiling was brightly lit by an immense chandelier of deer antlers. Brynn hadn't seen a rustic building so impressive since her dad had taken her to the Old Faithful Inn in Yellowstone National Park when she was seven.

"You remember Jared," Rand said. "This is Brynn, tiger. She helped us when you were sick."

"Hey, Jared. I brought you a present." She held the teddy bear toward the boy.

One wide hazel eye filled with skepticism peeked out at her. She wiggled the toy to animate it and said in a high squeaky voice, "Hi, Jared. I'm Officer Friendly."

Jared raised his head and gazed at the bear. "Who?"

"I protect you from all the bad guys," Brynn explained in the same funny tone. "Will you play with me?"

"That voice alone must strike fear in the hearts of evildoers," Rand said with a bone-melting grin.

"Evildoers?" Brynn asked in her normal voice, no mean feat considering the effect Rand's smile was having on her pulse rate.

"Legal term," Rand answered with a straight face. "We lawyers use it all the time."

Jared stretched out a hand, and Brynn gave him the bear. He clutched it fiercely against his chest and buried his face in the toy's plush fur.

"Hi, Ossifer Fwienly," he murmured, mutilating the name in typical toddlerese.

"What do you say to Brynn?" Rand prompted gently.

Jared shot her a quick glance before hiding his face in the toy again. "Thank you."

"You're welcome, sweetie." Brynn was happy he appeared much healthier than the last time she'd seen him. "You feeling okay now?"

Without looking at her, he nodded, his withdrawal almost painful to observe. Brynn had encountered shy children before, but Jared's quiet attitude went beyond simple timidness. She sensed an underlying sadness and wondered where the two-year-old's parents were.

Footsteps sounded from the rear of the hall, and a short, plump woman with gray hair in a pixie cut and rosy-pink cheeks hurried toward them, wiping her hands on her apron.

"Sorry, Rand," the woman said in a lilting voice with the faintest trace of Irish brogue. "I was headed for the door, but the oven timer went off, and I didn't want the salmon overcooked."

Rand smiled at the older woman with obvious affection. "No problem. Lillian O'Mara, meet Brynn Sawyer."

"Hi," Brynn said. "Whatever you're cooking smells good."

"It's nice to meet a friend of Rand's," Lillian said with a welcoming twinkle in her green eyes. "I've known him and Patrick since they were both no bigger than this little one." Lillian held out her arms to Jared. "Come to Lillian, darlin'. It's past your bedtime."

Jared released his stranglehold on Rand and went willingly to Lillian, but hid his face again as soon as he'd transferred to her arms.

"I'll tuck him in and sing him to sleep. By then, dinner will be ready." Crooning softly to the child, Lillian climbed the spectacular log staircase and disappeared into the upper reaches of the huge house.

"How about a drink?" Rand gestured toward his right, motioning Brynn into a living room with the same soaring timber-framed ceiling as the foyer. Walls of glass revealed the abundance of exterior lighting that showcased the surrounding decks and landscape. A fireplace of mountain stone, large enough to roast an ox, blazed with a cheery fire.

"Nice place," Brynn said, and struggled to suppress another cringe. So far she was two-for-two on the road to striking out in the game of scintillating conversation. "Plenty of room for the three of you."

"Lillian lives in the guest house," Rand explained. "About that drink?"

"Fine."

He crossed the room and opened a set of doors built into the wall next to the fireplace to hide a fully stocked bar. "What would you like?"

Nothing to further addle her already befuddled senses. "Do you have a Diet Coke?"

"Sure." He placed ice in a tumbler and poured her Diet Coke, then fixed himself a scotch on the rocks. When he handed her the glass, their fingers brushed briefly, sending a buzz of pleasant warmth up her arm. He lifted his drink. "To friendship."

"To truth," Brynn countered and took a sip.

He stared intently for an instant, as if trying to assess her thoughts, and gestured to a sectional sofa covered in butter-soft beige leather. Brynn took a seat.

Rand settled across from her in the sofa's right angle. "You don't trust me, do you?"

She shrugged. "Trust has to be earned. I don't know you well enough to know if you deserve to be trusted."

"Ouch. Are you always so blunt?" Although his words were accusing, he hadn't lost his killer smile.

"Bluntness saves time." She sipped her drink and glanced around the massive room. Marion had said the house needed work, but what Brynn had seen looked fine. Mostly lots of window glass, aged timbers and minimal furnishings. "I don't like beating around the bush."

"An admirable attitude for you, but not very productive for a man who earns his living by running up billable hours." Rand reclined with one arm extended on the back of the sofa and swirled the ice in his glass with his other hand.

"So why am I here?" Brynn had already established her penchant for bluntness. She might as well exploit it.

Rand's smile faded, and his expression turned serious, drawing her attention to the accentuated planes of his high cheekbones. With the rugged attractiveness and deep tan of an athlete, he lacked the softness she expected from a man who spent his life in conference rooms and courthouses. Flames from the massive fireplace reflected in the deep brown of his eyes.

"As I explained before," Rand said, "I wanted to thank you."

She shook her head. "You already have."

He set his drink on a table behind the sofa and leaned toward her, his strong hands clasped between his knees. "Not enough. I could never thank you enough. I was out of my head with worry the night you pulled me over. If you hadn't stopped me, I might have killed Jared, myself and God knows who else."

The sincerity in his rich voice and the intensity of his gratitude threatened to crack the shell she'd thrown around her emotions. "Just doing my job. Protect and serve."

His gaze turned curious. "Why did you choose police work?"

"My dad's a cop, so it runs in the family. And I like people."

"But you don't like me?"

After eight years on the job, not much could surprise Brynn, but Rand's out-of-the-blue question definitely had. "What gives you that idea?"

He smiled again, his expression even more charming than before. "Your avoiding me like the plague was my first clue."

"But I'm here now." On the contrary, she found him too easy to like, but she wasn't about to admit it. She tensed, afraid she might reveal too much of her true feelings to a man clearly adept at cross-examination. "And I don't really know you well enough to know if I like you yet."

"Then that's another good reason for your being here tonight. To find out."

"Sounds like I don't have the corner on bluntness." She took a drink of Diet Coke and stared at the leaping flames to avoid his gaze.

"Why don't you like lawyers?" His question caught her off guard.

She fumbled for an answer that wouldn't sound rude. "What makes you think I don't?"

"As a litigator, I've learned to read jurors. That skill carries over into daily life. I noted your reaction when I said I was an attorney. It wasn't exactly positive."

"My experiences with attorneys haven't been exactly positive, either."

"Or with New Yorkers?"

"Guilty as charged."

Damn, the man was good. Was there nothing he'd

missed? She'd have to tread carefully. The last thing she wanted was Rand's observing how clearly she was attracted to him. But, she reminded herself, after tonight, once she'd satisfied her curiosity, her reactions and his observations would be moot points, because she wouldn't see him again. She had absolutely no use for a man in her life, didn't have time, especially for a man who rattled her as Rand did. Her job, as always, came first and required one hundred and fifty percent of her concentration.

Reminding herself that she had come to River Walk only to solve a puzzle, she quickly changed the subject. If Rand was an expert in cross-examination, she was no slouch at interrogation, either. Recalling Lillian's words, she asked, "Who's Patrick?"

Rand shuddered slightly, like a man in intense pain. "My brother and Jared's father."

"Is he in New York?"

Rand shook his head, his eyes almost black with sorrow. "Patrick is dead."

Chapter Four

"I'm sorry." Brynn's sympathy sounded genuine.

Rand reached for his drink and took a long swallow in hope that the scotch's numbing effect would kick in quickly. "It's been five months…"

"And it still hurts as if it were yesterday," Brynn supplied. Understanding glistened in her remarkable dark eyes.

"You know?"

"My mother died when I was four. Healing from that kind of loss takes a long time."

Sorrow etched a furrow in his forehead. "I'm finding that out."

"Where's Jared's mother?"

Rand sighed. "It's hardest on him, of course. He lost both his parents. Patrick and Joan spent a weekend at a country inn in Vermont last October. They were returning home to the city when a deer sprang onto the highway in front of their car. Patrick swerved to avoid it and hit a tree. He and Joan died instantly."

"Were you and Jared close before the accident?" Brynn said.

"No."

Guilt gnawed at him. For the past fifteen years, Rand had made a point of not being close to anyone. He'd been ruthless about his career, never allowing emotions or family obligations to slow his climb up the corporate ladder. He'd kept his eye on the prize, a senior partnership in Steinman, Slagle and Crump, the most prestigious law firm in Manhattan, and he hadn't permitted distractions. His guilt increased with the knowledge that even his move to Pleasant Valley dovetailed with his long-range ambitions.

He hadn't always been so calculating. He'd fallen wildly in love his second year in law school. He and Sharon had planned to work for the public defender's office and save the world once they graduated. When Sharon dumped him and he'd almost flunked out in his despair, he'd vowed never to let feelings rule him again. The best revenge, he'd decided, was living well, and over the past decade, he'd lived better than most men, making more money than he had time to spend.

"When my mother died," Brynn was saying, "I was really close to my dad. Losing her was hard, but without my father, it would have been even tougher. Coping with the loss of both parents must be really difficult for Jared."

"One of the reasons we came to Pleasant Valley," Rand said, "is so Jared and I will have plenty of time together. I want him to know he has someone who loves him and is here for him."

Brynn nodded. "And the other reason?"

Rand sat very still. Did she know, he wondered? One wrong word, one careless look, one guilty gesture would give him away. He said nothing, but raised his eyebrows in question.

"*One* of the reasons, you said before," Brynn elaborated. "Why else did you pick Pleasant Valley?"

"The country air," Rand said quickly. He was glad for at least one other truthful excuse. "I hope it will be good for Jared's health."

Brynn stared thoughtfully into her glass, then raised her gaze to his. She wore her shoulder-length hair, a soft cloud of auburn, loose around her face. God, she was a gorgeous woman, but didn't seem aware of that beauty at all.

"Why not Arizona?" she asked, "or Montana? I hear both those climates are healthy."

"Why are you so curious?" he asked with a laugh. "Do you work part-time for the Pleasant Valley chamber of commerce?"

"No," she admitted with a curve of her lips that formed an enticing dimple in her left cheek. "But Uncle Bud is president of the chamber. He's always interested in why people move to our area. Probably because newcomers are so rare. There're not many job opportunities here. A lot of our young people move away to find work."

Rand cast about for an explanation that would give nothing away. "When I was surfing the real estate sites on the Web, looking for country properties, I was struck by pictures of River Walk." That much, at least, was true. "Once I saw the place, I had to have it."

"You bought it without seeing it in person?"

"Had a virtual tour," Rand said hastily. "Almost as good as the real thing."

Brynn shook her head. "For all you knew, there could have been a factory spewing smoke on your back property line and a major highway outside your front door."

"I had a good real estate agent. He knew exactly what I wanted and made certain that River Walk fit the bill."

The conversation was veering dangerously close to topics Rand couldn't discuss. Luckily, Lillian chose that moment to announce dinner.

He pushed to his feet, held out a hand to Brynn and tugged her beside him. Surprised when she didn't pull away, he kept her hand in his all the way to the dining room until he pulled out her chair at a corner of the table, hewn from a massive four-foot-wide log from a tree that Rand had no hope of identifying.

He took a seat at the head of the table, and Lillian brought their plates from the kitchen. She placed an open bottle of Chardonnay at his elbow. "Anything else you'll be needing?" she asked.

Rand shook his head. "Everything's perfect. We can take care of ourselves, Lillian. Go put your feet up. You've had a long day."

"Good night, then."

"Good night, Lillian, and thank you," Brynn said.

Lillian left through the door to the kitchen. As Rand poured wine in Brynn's glass, he heard the back door close.

"She seems like a nice lady," Brynn observed.

"Lillian's a lifesaver. She was nanny to both Patrick and me, and she's come out of retirement to take care of Jared."

"A good cook, too." Brynn savored a bite of salmon in dill sauce that Lillian had served with steamed asparagus and russet potatoes.

"So," Rand said, "tell me about Pleasant Valley." He'd done his homework and studied the area thoroughly but wanted to enjoy Brynn's voice, as melodic and soothing as the sound of the river tumbling over the rocks below. In addition, the less he talked, the less likely he was to say more than he intended.

"Not much to tell," she responded with a shrug of her very pretty shoulders. "Nothing much ever happens here, although we did almost lose downtown when the river flooded last summer." She must have noted the concern in his eyes, because she added hastily, "But River Walk was never in any danger. The lowest deck was underwater for a day or so, but the house itself sits well above the flood plain."

"So my real estate agent assured me. Have you lived here all your life?"

Brynn nodded. "Most families in the valley have been here for generations." Her face glowed with enthusiasm, deepening the apricot color in her cheeks as she warmed to her topic. "Our ancestors fought alongside the Over Mountain Men, who passed through the valley on their way from Tennessee, in the Revolutionary War battles of King's Mountain and Cowpens."

"And in the Civil War?"

Her smile widened, revealing perfect white teeth. "You mean the War of Northern Aggression? My great-grandmother always insisted there was nothing civil about that war."

Best to avoid that conflict altogether, he decided. "What about the valley today? How would you describe it?"

She thought for a moment. "Rural, agricultural. Mostly small family farms where folks work hard to eke out a living."

"And the town?"

"A close-knit community. Take last summer's flood, for instance. Everybody young and old turned out to fill sandbags to hold back the river from the shops on the main street. The town population is small, mostly business owners, teachers, the staff at the medical center."

"No theaters? Restaurants?" Not that he was accustomed to night life—he was usually working—but with his present assignment, Rand anticipated time on his hands.

"Jodie's Café is open for breakfast and lunch," Brynn explained. "And Ridge's place on the Carsons Corner highway has the best barbecue in the Upstate. And a jukebox. Do you like country music?"

Music.

The word triggered a childhood memory of Patrick and him, stiff and uncomfortable in their best clothes, sitting on rigid straight chairs with their feet dangling above the floor while a string quartet from Julliard played Bach in the conservatory of his parents' estate in the Hamptons. He'd endured dozens of such performances, causing him to associate music with discomfort, boredom and an overwhelming desire to be elsewhere.

"I'm not much of a music fan," he admitted.

"Really?" She leaned her head to one side and studied him closely. "Let me guess."

"What?"

"What you do for fun."

Fun? He couldn't tear his gaze from her full lips or keep himself from thinking how enjoyable kissing them would be. Now *that* would be fun. "I'm a workaholic."

"So even when you play, it's work," Brynn said with an accuracy that stunned him. If she read him so well, he'd have to be very, very careful.

"I'll bet you're ruthless on the tennis court," she continued. "Or is it handball?"

"Handball," he admitted. "And I do play to win."

"Ever fished?" she asked.

He shook his head. "Never could see the point."

She laughed and the sound reminded him again of the river singing over stones below the house. "There is no point."

He stared at her, his fork halfway to his mouth. "I don't understand."

"Fishing is a wonderful excuse to be outdoors, enjoy nature and do absolutely nothing. Doesn't matter if you catch anything." Her expression was teasing. "You should try it. River Walk's the perfect spot."

"If you'll join me."

She shook her head. "You miss the best part if you don't fish alone."

"How so?"

"All alone, just you, the outdoors, the river and your thoughts. You get to know yourself better."

Rand shook his head. The prospect of being alone with his thoughts made him uncomfortable. He'd rather be buried in work, so he didn't have time to think.

"Forget fishing, then," Brynn said. "But you said last week, you're on sabbatical. You have to do something. Do you plan to remodel River Walk?"

"I might make a few changes. Do you know a good contractor?"

"You're not doing it yourself?"

"Can't tell one end of a hammer from another," Rand confessed.

"Too bad." Brynn gave an exaggerated sigh.

"Why?"

Her eyes sparked with mischief. "Men in tool belts are very sexy."

"Hmmm, let's see if I have this straight. You think a guy with a tool belt, sweat-stained undershirt, beer gut, chewing a cigar—"

"Stop, please." Brynn feigned dismay. "You've just ruined one of my best fantasies."

"Sorry." He raised his eyebrows in a leer. "But I'd love to hear the rest of them."

She shook her head. "A girl has to have some secrets."

Surprisingly, he found himself wishing he knew what Brynn's secrets were. For too long, he'd viewed the women he'd spent time with as means to an end, either to enhance his social image, a source of useful information or a pleasant but meaningless roll in the hay. Brynn was different. He wanted to know about her, simply for the sheer pleasure of her company.

He cleared their plates and brought in coffee and slices of the cake Lillian had baked for dessert.

Unlike so many model-thin women he'd escorted in New York, Brynn didn't pick at her dessert, but enjoyed every bite. When she finished, she picked up her coffee cup and shot him a glance over its rim. "Do you like to read?"

"Read?"

"Mysteries, science fiction, action/adventure thrillers?"

"Law books are my only reading."

She shook her head. "Unless you set up a satellite office here, you're in for a very dull time in Pleasant Valley."

Satellite office hit too close to home. Affecting nonchalance, he took the opening she'd offered. "I like to explore."

"Not much to explore here."

"Maybe not for you. You know this entire area like the back of your hand. But it's all new to me."

"You're serious?" Her expression was dubious.

"I've spent most of my life in an office," he said, warming to his subject and his subterfuge, "and I'm looking forward to spending time outdoors. If you had a friend arrive who'd never seen the valley, where's the first place you'd take him?"

"Archer Farm," she replied instantly.

He clamped his jaws to keep from blurting his astonishment. A rehabilitation center for juvenile delinquents was first on her sightseeing list? Strange choice. "What's so special about Archer Farm?" he asked, pretending ignorance.

"It's a special place with special people. Jeff Davidson has turned his old homestead into a haven where teenage boys at risk of being sent to prison have a chance to turn their lives around."

"By farming?" He didn't have to pretend this time. Rand's doubt that such a scheme could work was entirely genuine.

"The boys do much more than farm," Brynn said. "But you'll need to see for yourself to understand."

"I'd like that. Will you take me there?"

Brynn thought for a moment. "If we take Jared, too."

Rand hesitated. "All those strange boys might frighten him."

"You don't have to worry. They're good kids." Her enthusiasm was unmistakable, from the light in her eyes to her eager smile.

He lifted one eyebrow skeptically. "Good kids with rap sheets?"

"The staff at the farm brings out the best in the boys," Brynn insisted. "Besides, Jared will love seeing the new chicks and ducklings. I've never met a child yet who can resist baby animals."

Rand couldn't figure Brynn out. Most women he'd encountered showed intense interest in his wealth and status, but Brynn appeared totally unimpressed. Aside from wondering how a New York attorney would pass his time in this Southern backwater town, her only concern was for Jared. Accustomed to women practically throwing themselves at his feet, Rand found Brynn a refreshing change. The fact that she was also his entry ticket into the tightly knit community was an added plus.

"You're right." he said. "An outing will be good for Jared. When do we go?"

"Saturday's my next day off."

"Ten o'clock?" Rand asked. "Jared and I will pick you up. Now, let me show you the rest of the place."

BRYNN STOOD on River Walk's lower deck and filled her lungs with the crisp, cool night air. Underneath the planking, the rushing waters of the river churned and splashed over massive boulders. Above, a sliver of silver moon hung in the cloudless sky. Behind her, River Walk rose like a mountain lodge featured in a travel brochure, its low-voltage lights emphasizing the rustic gabled architecture and the blue spruce, Japanese maples and redbud trees, bursting with delicate lavender blossoms, that accented the meticulously groomed landscape.

Beside her, Rand leaned his elbows on the deck railing and stared into the river. A light breeze swirled around them, teasing her with the scent of his leather jacket, the clean fresh scent of soap and his unmistakable and entirely pleasant aura of masculinity. A movie director couldn't have set a more romantic scene with the moon above, the river below and one very handsome leading man beside her.

The only thing out of place was Brynn.

She felt strange in such a romantic scenario. It was time she started acting and thinking like a cop. She'd come to River Walk to solve a puzzle, and, while she'd found answers to her initial questions, she'd discovered Rand Benedict more a mystery than ever. He'd purchased a place on a river, famous for trout fishing, but he didn't like to fish. He apparently had no interests other than work, but he was taking a sabbatical. And beneath his confident exterior, she glimpsed a loneliness as deep as little Jared's. She was adding two and two and only coming up with three. What had she missed?

"Where are Jared grandparents?" she asked.

Rand grinned in the moonlight. "Back to being blunt, are we?"

She shrugged. "A single uncle doesn't usually end up as his nephew's guardian, not when there're women in the family."

"My parents live in Paris—"

"France?"

He nodded. "Father worked there in international banking. They liked the city so much, they retired there. And Jared's a handful for people my parents' age."

"What about Jared's maternal grandmother?"

Rand frowned. "Joan's father has Alzheimer's, and her mother already has more than she can handle."

"So it's Uncle Rand to the rescue?"

He turned and leaned against the railing to face her. "I admit, I'm in totally over my head. I can safeguard Jared's legal interests, but I'm clueless where raising children is concerned. Thank God for Lillian. I need all the help I can get."

Moonlight reflected in his deep brown eyes, reminding her of silver wrappers on chocolate Kisses.

"I can only sympathize," she admitted. "I haven't had much experience myself."

"Are you kidding? You're the first stranger Jared's responded to without hysterical screams. And I watched you in action with that third grade class. You're a natural around children."

She shook her head, pleased at his compliment but aware of her lack of expertise. "If you want advice about children, you should ask Jodie when we visit Archer Farm. She raised Brittany alone for fourteen years before she married Jeff Davidson."

As soon as the words left her mouth, Brynn reconsidered her advice. Ever since Brittany had hit puberty, she'd been hell on wheels, often driving her mother to tears of frustration. "Or better yet, you can talk to Gofer."

Rand looked surprised. "Gopher, as in animal?"

Brynn laughed and shook her head. "Jack Hager's

favorite expression is 'go for broke,' so his friends call him Gofer. He's the resident psychologist at Archer Farm."

"I may need a shrink to get through this," Rand said, but only partially in jest. "And friends."

The appeal in his voice touched her. And Brynn didn't want to be affected. Certainly not by a man with whom she had absolutely nothing in common. Yes, he was drop-dead good-looking, but her daddy had taught her long ago that beauty was only skin deep. She knew nothing else about Rand except that he was a New York lawyer who would return north as soon as he'd bonded with his orphaned nephew. Neither of those facts boded well for anything other than the most casual friendship. She'd agreed to show him Archer Farm, partly because she enjoyed his company, but mainly for Jared's sake. After that, the Yankee stranger was on his own.

"I have to go," she said. "I have an early shift in the morning."

Without another comment, Rand walked with her to her car and opened the door for her.

"Thanks for dinner," she said.

"Where do you live?"

"Why?" Lordy, she hoped he wasn't going to keep following her.

"If I'm picking you up Saturday, I have to know where."

The man had her so flustered, she'd jumped to the

wrong conclusion and forgotten she hadn't given directions. "211 Mountain Street. It runs parallel to
Piedmont Avenue one block north."

"I'll see you Saturday at ten." He leaned down
and brushed her cheek with his lips. "Thank-you
again, Brynn, for all your help."

Shaken by the unexpected gesture, she climbed
into the driver's seat, closed the door and circled the
driveway toward the road. Her face burned where his
lips had touched her, and she was all too aware of
Rand's silhouette, clearly visible in her rearview
mirror, as he watched her depart.

RAND WAITED until the taillights of Brynn's SUV
disappeared around a curve in the drive before entering the house. Switching off lights as he went, he
mounted the stairs to the second floor. At the door
to Jared's room, he paused. A faint night-light illumi-
nated the sleeping child, who hugged his new teddy
bear in his sleep.

Patrick's voice from the night Jared was born
rang in Rand's memory. "My son won't be raised
like we were," his brother had declared.

"Rich and spoiled?" Rand had said with a grin.

"You know what I mean. Mother and Father never
paid any attention to us, except when Lillian dressed
us up and dragged us out for inspection when company came. Jared's going to spend lots of time with
his mom and dad and know that they love him."

A knot formed in Rand's throat. He'd spent too little time with his brother, especially during the past fifteen years, and now those opportunities were gone for good. And Patrick was forever unable to fulfill his vow to his son.

I'll do my best, Patrick, but I'm a sorry substitute for you.

Rand stepped into the room and approached the bed. Jared's breathing was easy, thank God, and he wasn't whimpering in his sleep, as he'd done so often since his parents had died. Rand experienced an unfamiliar tightness in his chest as he watched the sleeping child.

He tucked a blanket gently around the boy and brushed his blond hair back from his forehead. "Sleep tight, tiger," he whispered softly. "Uncle Rand is here if you need him."

He padded quietly from the room and went into the study next to the master bedroom. At the large desk, he unrolled a plat map, secured it with paperweights and leaned over to study the areas outlined in red. The Bickerstaff property next to Archer Farm, over one thousand prime acres, and farther west, nearer town, Mauney's dairy farm, with nine hundred acres, were his targeted goals.

The first time Rand had seen this map was a month ago in the inner sanctum of Charles Steinman's office. Rand had answered his boss's summons to find Steinman and another man pouring over the plat map, spread across his boat-sized desk.

"Rand," Steinman had greeted him with fake heartiness, "meet Gus Farrington."

Rand clasped Gus's outstretched hand. "Of Farrington Properties?"

Farrington shot Steinman a pleased look, and Steinman all but burst his trademark red suspenders in a proud preen. "See, I told you he'd be up to speed."

Farrington nodded. "I need someone sharp. That incompetent nitwit from Fitzhugh and Worth ruined my last deal."

"How can I help?" Rand asked.

Farrington poked a finger at a red outline on the plat map. "Buy me this property."

Rand looked from Farrington to Steinman. "That seems simple enough."

Farrington sighed and dropped into a chair. "You'd think so, wouldn't you?"

Steinman waved Rand to a seat next to Farrington and settled behind his desk. "If we can deliver, Gus will switch his entire account to us."

Rand nodded and managed to keep the glee from his expression. Farrington Properties was developing retirement villages with their own megamalls all over the country. Garnering their account would be a huge coup for the law firm and maybe earn Rand the senior partnership to which he aspired.

"Someone from Fitzhugh and Worth tried to buy this before?" Rand nodded toward the map.

Farrington uttered a disgusted sound. "Not this piece. We sent their representative down to Westminster, South Carolina, to look at two thousand acres that border Lake Tugaloo. There were several separate parcels we wanted him to acquire discreetly, but the bumbling idiot let the cat out of the bag. Before we knew it, we had the environmentalists and preservationists lined up against us on one side, and on the other, those willing to sell had jacked their prices so high that buying would have wiped out our profit margin."

"So this—" Rand squinted at the map "—Pleasant Valley is your backup plan."

Farrington nodded. "Every day, baby boomers are retiring by the thousands and moving south. This area of South Carolina is ripe for developing retirement communities, and the accompanying malls will bring jobs to the locals who've lost work in the textile industry to cheaper labor overseas."

Farrington had seemed convinced his development would be good for the valley. And Brynn had admitted tonight that life was hard for farmers here. As a result, both Eileen Bickerstaff and Joe Mauney should be anxious to sell. If so, his job would be a piece of cake and over in a few weeks.

But the memory of Brynn's expression when she talked about her tightly knit community raised warning flags in his mind. What if neither property owner accepted his offer?

And why now, after only a few hours with Brynn, did Rand feel sudden misgivings and even guilt about the job he'd come here to do?

Chapter Five

Brynn sank into the chair at the Hair Apparent for her scheduled Friday afternoon appointment. Amy Lou Baker floated a pink nylon cape over her shoulders and tied it around her neck. Standing behind her, Amy Lou spoke to Brynn's reflection in the room-length mirror that ran above the counter with a deep sink and the combs, brushes and rollers of Amy Lou's trade.

"Sugar, you have got hair to die for." Amy Lou gently deconstructed Brynn's French braid and ran her fingers like a comb through the thick strands. "If I could match and bottle this color, I'd make me enough money to live high on the hog."

Brynn smiled at the woman who'd cut her hair her entire life. "Thank goodness it's darkened since I was a kid. I hated being called Carrottop."

"Nobody's going to call you names now, unless it's Hey, Good-Lookin'. Specially with that big gun you carry all the time."

Amy Lou laughed with delight at her own joke, rotated Brynn's chair and leaned her backward over the sink for a shampoo. The warm water and gentle massage of Amy Lou's fingertips eased Brynn's weary muscles, and the patter of the beautician's constant chatter washed over her like the spray from the sink nozzle.

Brynn had fuzzy memories of first coming to the Hair Apparent with her mother, and, except for a few more lines in her face, Amy Lou hadn't changed much in almost thirty years. Her hair was still the same extraordinary honey-blond, she still wore too much makeup, the same pink polyester uniforms and sensible white shoes, and she still talked non-stop from the time Brynn stepped through the door of the shop until her departure. But Amy Lou's heart was as expansive as her teased hairdo, and she, like so many other women in town, including Sophie Nathan and Cat Stratton, Jodie's and Merrilee's mothers, had served as wonderful surrogate maternal figures in Brynn's life.

Amy Lou shut off the taps, squeezed the excess moisture from Brynn's hair and wrapped her head turban-style in a thick towel. With an expert flick of her wrist, she propped the chair upright and whirled Brynn until she once more faced the mirror.

"What'll it be today, sugar? The usual?"

Brynn nodded.

Amy Lou's aging face wrinkled in thought. "You

sure? I can give you an upswept style with lots of dangly curls. Something real romantic."

"Which my uniform cap would destroy the first time I put it on."

"Pshaw," Amy Lou said with a frown. "How're you going to catch a man without baiting the trap?"

"The only men I need to catch," Brynn said, "are those with warrants for their arrests. And I can assure you, *they* don't give a rip about my hair."

Amy Lou rubbed Brynn's wet hair hard with the towel, as if to drive home her point. "You're too busy taking care of everybody else, sugar. Checking on old folks like Mrs. Bickerstaff and Mrs. Weatherstone. You deliver their groceries and drive them to their doctors or here to have their hair done. And when you're not doing that, you're riding herd on those wild boys at Archer Farm. You need to take care of yourself."

Brynn purposely misunderstood. "I do take care of myself. I watch my weight and get plenty of exercise and sleep."

Like a terrier with a bone, Amy Lou was not about to be sidetracked. She picked up her comb and scissors and cut straight to the chase. "When's the last time you were kissed, sugar?"

Night before last.

Just thinking about her evening with Rand turned her insides all warm and fluttery, the same sensation Brynn remembered from Christmas mornings as a child, waiting to see what Santa had left beneath the tree. But a simple buss on the cheek didn't count as a real kiss. And since Amy Lou delivered better news coverage than the *County Chronicle,* Brynn wasn't about to admit to her pseudokiss from the attractive lawyer.

The best defense was a good offense. "What about you, Amy Lou? It's been seven years since Harold died. Ever thought about marrying again?"

Amy Lou's eyes moistened. "When you've had the perfect husband, you can never find another man who'll fill his shoes."

Her declaration spoke volumes for the power of love. Harold Baker hadn't been exactly Brynn's idea of the consummate spouse. He had worked at Jay-Jay's garage, and Brynn could still picture him, built like a brick outhouse with grease on his coveralls and under his fingernails, a man of few words, who drank too much. But he'd treated Amy Lou like a queen, and they'd been a model loving couple until cancer from the cigarettes he'd smoked since the age of thirteen had claimed his life.

Amy Lou sniffed and cleared her throat. "I hear you've met the new owner of River Walk."

Brynn wasn't surprised. The Hair Apparent was Pleasant Valley's communications central. Every tidbit of gossip concerning the town and valley either originated or was disseminated within the shop's pale pink walls. "I met him at the hospital last week. His nephew was ill."

"I heard he asked you out."

Brynn closed her eyes. Of course the children in Mrs. Shepherd's class had reported Rand's request to speak with her privately to their mothers, who had drawn their own conclusions and who also all had their hair done by Amy Lou. Brynn, hoping to minimize the gossip, met Amy Lou's gaze and said with all the nonchalance she could muster, "Mr. Benedict invited me to dinner to thank me for helping take his nephew to the hospital. And I wanted to see how little Jared was doing, so I took him a teddy bear out to River Walk."

"This Mr. Benedict have a first name?"

"Rand, uh, Randall."

"He single?"

"Yes, but—"

"Good-lookin'?"

Brynn pretended to take a moment to think. "Not bad."

"Well, there you go." Amy Lou lifted a strand of wet hair and whacked like a sartorial samurai. "Maybe you should get to know him. Have yourself some fun."

"He won't be here long. As soon as he's spent some time getting better acquainted with his orphaned nephew, they're going back to New York."

"Men have been known to change their minds." Amy Lou moved to Brynn's other side and snipped some more.

"Wouldn't matter if he did," Brynn insisted. "Rand Benedict and I have absolutely nothing in common."

Amy Lou's eyes twinkled. "You're a woman, he's a man. What more do you need?"

"He's a lawyer. And a Yankee."

Amy Lou caught her gaze in the mirror and held it tight. "You give lip service to those pet peeves of yours, but, sugar, you can't fool me. I know you've always judged folks by what's in their hearts, not where they're from or what they do, no matter how many jokes you tell."

I'm busted, Brynn thought. Amy Lou knew her too well. "I have to complain about something."

"Of course, sugar. Everybody does. With me, it's my bunions. I should never have worn those pointy-toed shoes in the sixties."

Brynn breathed a sigh of relief when Amy Lou changed the subject. The beautician could ramble on about her sore feet for hours.

But, breaking from habit, Amy Lou switched subject midstream. "I think you ought to give that Yankee lawyer a chance. He might turn out to be 'a real good man.'" She sang the last few words in a parody of Tim McGraw, her favorite country vocalist, and performed a spirited two-step, despite her bunions.

"Doesn't matter if he is a real good man. Rand Benedict and I are as different as night and day. If you meet him, you'll know instantly what I mean."

"Opposites attract, sugar," Amy Lou said with a knowing grin. She set her scissors down and flipped the blow-dryer on high, effectively drowning out further protests.

Brynn closed her eyes again, afraid Amy Lou might read her thoughts. Rand was definitely her opposite and Brynn did find him enticingly attractive. And Amy Lou had a point about having fun. Brynn's best friends, Merrilee and Jodie, were spending most of their free time with their husbands. And Brynn wasn't interested in hooking up with a local man with serious intentions. If all she wanted was a spring fling, Rand, with his cultural, economic and regional differences and imminent departure, would be an interesting—and safe—diversion.

SATURDAY MORNING, Rand pulled the Jaguar to the curb in front of Brynn's Arts and Crafts–style bungalow on tree-lined Mountain Street. Built around the 1920s, the house was one of the newer structures in the quiet neighborhood of mostly Victorian-style residences. Unlike the cheek-by-jowl buildings of newer developments throughout the country, these older homes were surrounded by sweeping green lawns, magnificent old trees and beds of colorful spring flowers. When the towering oaks and maples that lined the streets leafed out, they'd provide a shady canopy against the coming summer heat. And when the weather warmed, Rand expected the homeowners would be sitting on their wide front porches this time of day, enjoying their coffee and morning paper.

Unlike New York City streets at this hour, which would be jammed with wall-to-wall people, no one was in sight in the residential area. But vehicular and pedestrian traffic had filled Pleasant Valley's main street a few minutes ago when Rand had passed through, and total strangers had lifted their hands in enthusiastic greetings and flashed him welcoming smiles as they went about their Saturday shopping.

Five minutes early for his ten o'clock rendezvous with Brynn, Rand rolled down the Jag's window. Clean, crisp air, devoid of gasoline fumes, the stench of rotting garbage and other noxious city smells, filled the car and carried the lilting trill of a mockingbird. Rand glanced back at Jared in his car seat, who clutched the teddy bear Brynn had given him and smiled at the call of the bird.

"Pwetty," his nephew said.

The boy's smile was a rare gift, lifting Rand's spirits. "It is, isn't it?"

The knot of tension loosened in Rand's gut. Until he'd come to this sleepy valley a few weeks ago, he hadn't realized what a pressure cooker he'd lived in. He was on a too-fast treadmill in his high-powered job with every conversation aimed at placing him higher on the ladder of success, every minute tightly scheduled in his day planner.

Here he didn't have to worry about keeping appointments or the impression he made. The people he'd met, from the doctors and nurses at the medical center to the clerks in the stores, appeared to accept him at face value. They showed no interest in what position he held or the money he'd made or what clubs he belonged to. Instead, they inquired whether he was comfortable in his new home and how Jared was doing, with no apparent ulterior motives other than genuine friendliness.

He could get used to these amiable neighbors and the blissful peacefulness. But he didn't dare. He'd be headed back to New York, the sooner, the better, and, if he pulled off this deal, the senior partnership he coveted would finally be his.

That thought tightened his gut again, and he wished he hadn't forgotten to bring along the antacids he'd been eating like candy for the past several years.

A screen door slammed, and he glanced up to see Brynn running down the walk. She moved with the easy, long-legged gait of an athlete, and her form-fitting jeans showed off the trim muscles of her thighs. A bulky pale blue sweater with the collar of a crisp white blouse peeking through at the neckline accented her sparkling dark blue eyes, and her hundred-watt smile made him catch his breath. Before he could move to open the door, she'd slid onto the front seat beside him.

"Hi," she said to him, then turned to Jared. "Hey, Jared, and hey to you, too, Officer Friendly."

For once, Jared didn't hide his face but smiled at Brynn shyly.

"He hasn't let go of that bear since you gave it to him," Rand said. "It's even had a bath."

"Really?" Brynn looked to Jared. "You put him in the tub?"

Jared nodded solemnly. "Wif me."

"Thank God for clothes dryers," Rand said. "The bear is apparently indestructible."

Brynn grinned at Jared, and the car seemed suddenly filled with sunshine. "That's what friends are for, to go everywhere with you, right?"

"Wight," the boy answered and smiled back.

The knot in Rand's gut loosened another notch at the boy's happy expression. Jared liked Brynn. *Hell,* Rand thought, *I like Brynn. More than I've liked anyone in a long, long time.* Today was going to be a good day.

"Nice house." Rand nodded toward Brynn's place. "Great architecture."

"Thanks." Her features softened with obvious affection for her home. "I grew up in that house."

"You live alone?"

Brynn shook her head. "With my dad. He's chief of police."

"He working today?" Rand wondered if her not inviting him in to meet her father was a bad sign.

"He's at an FBI seminar in Quantico. When he gets home, he can tell you all about River Walk's history. He knew the original owners."

"I'll look forward to that." Rand started the engine. "So how do we get to Archer Farm?"

"Straight ahead four blocks, then hang a left. That'll put you back on Valley Road."

"Do they know we're coming?" Rand asked.

"I spoke with Jodie yesterday. Her husband Jeff is the farm's administrator. They're expecting us."

Enjoying the attractive homes and gardens of the historic district, Rand drove slowly through the neighborhood, followed Brynn's directions and turned onto the highway. As the Jaguar picked up speed, he glanced at Brynn. "Tell me about Archer Farm. Has it been here long?"

He knew the basic facts from his research but wanted to hear more about the people connected with the unusual project.

"Jeff Davidson grew up there," Brynn said, "but the farm was little more than a rundown house and barn then. The only crop was illegal moonshine that Jeff's father produced from a still up the mountain. Jeff's mother died when he was a baby, and he had a rough life, raised by Hiram, who was mean when drunk and seldom sober. As a result, Jeff was a loner and a hell-raiser."

"And this same Jeff is rehabilitating at-risk teenage boys?" Rand shook his head in amazement.

Brynn nodded. "As soon as Jeff was old enough, he left the valley and joined the Marines. The Corps became the family he'd never had, taught him discipline, gave him focus. Four of the staff members at Archer Farm are former Marines, too. Last spring, they helped Jeff build the boys' dormitory and refurbish the house and barn."

"So it's too soon to tell if the project's a success?"

"You can judge for yourself, but from my point of view, Jeff and his team have worked miracles."

Rand experienced an irrational twinge of jealousy and cut her a searching glance. "Sounds like you're fond of this Jeff."

"I am. He's married to one of my best friends. In fact, I was on my way home from their wedding reception at the farm when I first met you and Jared."

The sun, high in the cloudless sky at their backs, cast a golden glow over the valley that seemed to float in the light green haze of early spring. To his left, the Piedmont River tumbled over rocks and boulders, creating a froth of white water. To his right, rolling meadows stretched toward the distant mountains. The deep green roof of a farmhouse, the peak of a red barn and twin grain silos were visible behind the crest of a hill.

"That's a beautiful place," Rand said.

"Joe Mauney's dairy farm. He works it with his son. It's been in their family for generations."

Rand's interest perked up at the Mauney name. The farm was one of the properties Farrington wanted. "Dairy farming must be hard work."

"The Mauneys put in long hours, up way before dawn for the first milking, then going from one chore to the next until the last milking at sunset." Brynn's voice held no tinge of sympathy. She was merely stating facts. "And cows don't know when it's Saturday or Sunday. They still have to be milked."

"Is it a big farm?"

"Almost a thousand acres," Brynn explained. "Has to be to support that many cows."

"The land alone must be worth a lot." Rand kept his expression neutral. "Bet they could sell it and make enough to retire."

"And do what?" Brynn's voice shot up an octave in surprise. "The Mauneys are dairy farmers. That's their life. They'd go nuts lounging on some Florida beach, twiddling their thumbs."

Rand shrugged. "They could learn to play golf."

Brynn hooted with laughter.

"What's so funny?"

"You haven't met the Mauneys. They're big, quiet men who love the solitude of the land and their cows. They'd enjoy golf and the pretensions that go with it about as much as a pig does a barbecue."

Although she'd just informed him how difficult this assignment might prove, he couldn't help smiling at her description. And, he realized with a jolt, he was actually enjoying himself. When was the last time *that* had happened?

The Jaguar rounded a curve in the road and approached a low, log building on the right. A line of cars and trucks stood in the parking lot out front.

"That's the veterinary clinic," Brynn said, then flushed an attractive shade of coral. "But you've probably read the sign a dozen times passing by on the way to River Walk."

"Looks like a busy place."

Brynn nodded. "Grant Nathan and Jim Stratton are the vets. Grant's the brother of Jodie, Jeff Davidson's wife. And Grant's wife Merrilee, Jim's daughter, is another of my best friends."

Rand shook his head in mock dismay. "I'll never be able to keep all these people and their relationships straight."

"Sure you—" Brynn stopped abruptly.

"What?"

"I started to say you'd get to know everyone after a while, but I don't suppose you'll be here long enough." She fixed him with an inquisitive stare and inquired with her characteristic bluntness, "How long will you be here?"

"Maybe longer than I'd planned."

Especially now that he knew the Mauneys wouldn't be anxious to sell. And with Brynn beside him and the beauty of the land unfolding around him, he wouldn't mind extending his stay. Remaining longer in the valley definitely held a growing attraction.

Chapter Six

"Ever thought about getting Jared a dog?" Brynn asked as they passed the vets' clinic.

"Isn't he a bit young for a pet?"

"Not if you get the right kind. A Lab is great with children. I had a Lab named Lucky when I was Jared's age. After my mother died, I used to curl up against him to sleep. He'd lick my face when I cried. Next to my dad, Lucky was my greatest comfort."

Brynn's suggestion had its appeal. Rand and Patrick had begged for a dog when they were kids, but their parents wouldn't hear of an animal in the house. Instead, the brothers first had ponies, then horses, kept in the stables at the Hamptons and ridden only under the most stringent supervision. The prospect of a dog, not only for Jared but also to accompany Rand on his treks along the riverbank, was tempting.

"Anyone raise Labs around here?" he asked.

"Not that I know of," Brynn replied, "but Grant can find you one on the Internet."

"Dogs by mail order? Do they ship them FedEx?"

Her laughter floated through the car, and when she shook her head, her light floral fragrance teased his nostrils. For a woman who could probably take down a two-hundred-fifty-pound drunk and cuff him, she had an alluringly feminine side, from her seductive scent and sensual curves to the magic shining in her eyes and the charming timbre of her voice.

"Most breeds have rescue programs," Brynn was saying. "If a dog's been abandoned or needs a new home when it's owner dies, rescue volunteers sometimes drive the animal cross-country in relays to its new owner. Grant found Mrs. Weatherstone—she's an elderly widow in town—a chihuahua through a rescue service when her old pet died. The dog came all the way from North Dakota."

"Doggie?" Jared said.

Brynn turned toward the back seat. "You like doggies?"

"Uh-huh…and Ossifer Fwienly."

"A dog would be great here at River Walk," Rand said, "but a Lab's a big pet for a city apartment."

"Aren't there dog walkers you could hire?"

"True," Rand conceded, still hesitant. Jared's arrival had made a major impact on Rand's formerly uncluttered and regimented life. The addition of a dog pushed him further toward domestication.

"I'll be glad to talk to Grant," Brynn said, "if you're interested."

"Do they ever rescue puppies?" Shoving aside his reservations, Rand relished the prospect of Jared with a puppy. Hell, he'd buy a whole zoo if it would make the boy laugh again.

"Grant will know."

"Maybe you can introduce me to Grant."

Brynn nodded. "Puppy or not, you should meet him and Merrilee. They're your nearest neighbors. And you and Merrilee have something in common. She lived six years in New York City."

Brynn launched into a description of Merrilee Nathan's photography career and her book of photos of country vets that was about to be published, but Rand was only halfway listening. He kept glancing at Jared in the rearview mirror and noting the welcome change in the boy's demeanor.

When Rand had taken custody five months ago, Jared had been withdrawn and miserably unhappy. He hadn't whined or cried, except for whimpering in his sleep. His chubby little face had held no animation, and nothing and no one had sparked the boy's interest. He'd been terrified of strangers but had accepted Lillian without protest, and seemed to find her presence comforting. But only Rand—and now Brynn—had been able to coax the occasional smile from the child.

Jared's unhappiness broke Rand's heart. He'd never spent time around children, barely knew his own nephew when Patrick died, but in the past few months, Rand had been amazed at the strength of his growing love for this little guy, who reminded him of Patrick at that age. More than anything, Rand wanted to see Jared run and laugh and play like a normal kid, to enjoy all the activities Rand and Patrick had been sheltered from as children, and above all, to know that he was safe and loved.

Something about Brynn had clicked with Jared. He sat in his car seat now, head cocked, eyes shining, engrossed in the sound of her voice. And earlier, miracle of miracles, she had made him laugh. Although she held little resemblance to Joan, maybe she reminded Jared of his mother. Whatever the reason, Rand was gratified to see Jared lose his little-boy-lost expression and was glad Brynn had insisted on bringing him today.

Rand drove past the turnoff that led to River Walk, and Brynn pointed to a road on the opposite side of the highway that took off to the right. "That's the entrance to Grant and Merrilee's house," she said.

Jared gazed out the window with apparent interest.

"Our neighbors live up that road, tiger," Rand said. "We should visit them soon."

"Okeedookie," Jared said unexpectedly. "Go visit."

"When you do," Brynn said, "just be alert for Gloria. Her size can be intimidating, but she's a sweetheart."

Rand pictured an Amazon in an apron. "Is Gloria the housekeeper?"

"Hah! More like the housewrecker, but only before Grant trained her. Besides, you'll soon learn that most folks around here don't have hired help. No, Gloria's another of Grant's rescues. An Irish wolfhound. Jared can ride her like a pony."

"Thanks for the heads-up." He thought for a moment. "If people in the valley don't have hired help, who took care of you while your father worked?"

"Usually the desk sergeant," Brynn said. "Dad fixed me a play area and a cot in a corner of his office and took me to work every day. If he had to go out, the duty officer kept an eye on me. Later, when I was older, I'd go to the station after school, until Dad was ready to go home."

"That must have been tough." Rand tried to imagine Brynn, just a couple of years older than Jared, spending her days in a police station."

"I loved it," Brynn said with genuine feeling, "being with my father all the time, plus a whole department of uncles in blue. Not to mention the women in town who'd drop in during the day to check on me. I had more attention than most kids with two parents." Her expression sobered and her voice dropped. "But I still missed my mother."

"No wonder you became a police officer."

She grinned. "Guess you could say I never wanted to leave home." She pointed up the road.

"There's another neighbor around the next curve you'll also enjoy meeting."

"Who's that?" Rand asked.

"Eileen Bickerstaff."

Bickerstaff's was the other property Farrington wanted Rand to acquire. He slowed the Jag as it approached another road leading off to the right and marked with a weathered sign.

"Blackberry Farm?" he queried. "Ms. Bickerstaff grows blackberries?"

"Not exactly. See those brambles on the fences along the road?"

Rand nodded.

"They grow wild, all over her property. In a few months, they'll be covered with plump ripe blackberries. Eileen picks them and makes jams, jellies, even wine."

Rand tried not to sound too interested. "Are blackberries her only crop?"

Brynn shook her head. "She also has apple and peach orchards, and she leases a few of her fields to the Mauneys for cultivation. At ninety-six, she's not as active as she used to be."

At that age, Rand thought, the woman would either be anxious to sell and move, maybe to an assisted living facility, or, worst-case scenario, determined to live out her life on her farm. "Does she live alone?"

"Yes. She's a remarkable woman. Her husband

died in World War II. They had no children, and she's operated Blackberry Farm pretty much on her own for the past sixty-some years."

"She sounds fascinating." Rand kept his eagerness from his voice. "I'd like to meet her."

"Better slow down," Brynn warned. "The road to Archer Farm is coming up on your left."

They had reached the western end of the valley, where the highway began its climb into the mountains. Rand almost didn't see the entrance to the gravel drive, partially hidden by the arching branches of rhododendron and mountain laurel, heavy with dark, glossy leaves and tight buds. He turned onto the road Brynn indicated and shifted into low gear to navigate the series of steep, sharp switchbacks that led up the mountainside. The drive passed through a thick forest of hardwoods, the brown and silver bark of their bare limbs glistening in the morning sun.

"Talk about the middle of nowhere," Rand muttered.

"Keeps the boys away from trouble," Brynn explained. "No cars to steal, no drugs to buy, no gangs to join. No dangerous temptations. The middle of nowhere has its advantages."

"You have a point."

At the next rise, the land flattened out where a multiacre plateau had been carved into the mountainside. Sunlight flooded the clearing and sparkled on the fresh white paint of a two-story farmhouse, the deep red of an ancient barn and a massive log building that dominated the space. An assortment of pickup trucks and SUVs filled the gravel parking lot.

An attractive, petite young woman in jeans and a pullover sweater and a tall muscular man in olive drab slacks and a sweatshirt emblazoned with USMC stepped off the farmhouse porch and headed down the walk as Rand parked.

Brynn climbed out of the car, and the woman greeted her with a hug. The man came around the Jag as Rand got out and offered Rand his hand.

"Welcome to Archer Farm," he said. "I'm Jeff Davidson. And this is my wife, Jodie."

Jeff with his bone-crunching grip was one hundred percent Marine, exuding strength and discipline, but his toughness was tempered by the love and pride in his eyes when he introduced his wife.

Jodie waved from the other side of the vehicle. "Glad you could come."

"Okay if I take Jared out?" Brynn asked him.

Rand hesitated. Jared was shy around everyone, particularly strangers, but one look at the excitement shining on the boy's face quelled Rand's doubts. "Sure."

Brynn reached into the back seat, unfastened the restraining straps on the carrier and lifted Jared in her arms. "Jared, this is Jodie."

"Hi, Jared," Jodie said in a gentle voice. "Who's your friend?"

Jared held up his bear. "Ossifer Fwienly. Bwynn bwinged him to me."

Brynn held the boy as naturally as if she carried children every day, and for once, Jared didn't hide his face but glanced eagerly around him.

"Do you like animals?" Jodie asked the boy.

"Uh-huh. Gots any beahs?"

"No bears," Jeff said, "but cows, horses, goats and chickens. Here comes Gofer now. He'll show you around."

A tall, blond man with friendly blue eyes and the same military bearing and apparel as Jeff hurried toward the group from the direction of the log dormitory.

"Hi, Brynn. Good to see you again," he said before turning to Rand. "I'm Jack Hager, but my friends call me Gofer."

"Rand Benedict." Rand shook his hand. "And that's my nephew, Jared."

"We have a ton of work to finish this morning," Jodie said in apology, "so I hope you won't mind if we don't accompany you. But we'd love to visit over lunch if you can stay."

Brynn looked to Rand. "It's your call."

Rand couldn't resist the exhilarating mountain air, the farm's serenity and the Davidsons' warm welcome—or the fact that remaining for lunch would extend his time with Brynn.

"If you're sure it's no trouble," he said to Jodie.

She laughed. "We always feed a crowd here. Believe me, three more mouths are no problem."

"Now," Jeff said, "if you'll excuse us, we'll see you at lunch." The couple went back into the house.

"Jeff's up to his neck in the end of the month paperwork," Gofer said. "The wedding and honeymoon put him behind, but with Jodie's help, he'll meet our deadlines. There's a lot of governmental red tape involved in running a place like this."

Rand grinned. "I'm an expert in red tape. I'm an attorney."

"Really?" Gofer slanted a look of surprise toward Brynn, who avoided his gaze. Apparently Brynn's aversion to lawyers was well known. "Ready for the fifty-cent tour?"

Brynn hoisted Jared higher on her hip and flashed Gofer a smile that caused a hitch in Rand's breathing. "You take the point, Gofer," she instructed. "Isn't that how you Marines say it?"

The big Marine grinned. "Yeah, but I doubt if we can sneak up on the goats. We don't have any cover between here and the meadow."

Rand and Brynn, carrying Jared, fell in step behind Gofer as he crossed the parking lot, skirted the barn and led them to a fenced pasture. The enclosure held a herd of goats, including several kids just a few weeks old. The adults munched contentedly on the lush grass and the kids frolicked on spindly legs. Watching, Jared giggled and clapped his hands with delight. At the far end of the meadow, ducks and ducklings waddled along the edge of a pond.

Rand soaked up the peacefulness like dry ground absorbs rain. With the warmth of the sun on his face and air with the crispness of fine wine filling his lungs, he felt the knot in his gut disappear entirely. Jared was smiling, the most intriguing woman he'd ever met stood at his side and all was right with the world.

The peace disintegrated briefly when a loud clatter emanated from the barn, followed by a stream of curses that turned the air blue.

"Excuse me," Gofer said. "Sounds like there's a problem in the dairy." The psychologist double-timed it toward the barn.

"I was wondering where the teens were," Rand said with a wry smile. "That one has quite a vocabulary."

Brynn set Jared on his feet, and he poked his hand over the lower rail of the fence. "C'mere, goats."

Holding Jared's other hand, she propped an elbow on the top rail and gazed back toward the buildings. "Daniel works Saturdays at Jodie's Café and Jason does chores for Mrs. Weatherstone in town. The other boys are here getting ready for Daffodil Days next weekend."

"Daffodil Days?"

"Pleasant Valley's spring festival. Piedmont Avenue, the main street, is blocked off Saturday and Sunday, and people come from all over the county to set up booths. They sell crafts, folk art, food and just plain junk. It's the Upstate's biggest flea market. It's even advertised on HGTV."

"What do the Archer Farm boys sell?"

Brynn nodded toward Gofer, who was hurrying back from the barn. "You'll find out during the rest of the tour."

"Sorry to rush off," Gofer said when he joined them, and Rand couldn't help noting that the man wasn't at all breathless after his long sprint. The former Marine must have kept up his physical training. "There was a crisis in the dairy, but everything's under control."

"Jared wants to see the baby chicks," Brynn said.

"Baby chicks, coming up," Gofer said.

Moments later, Rand wished for a video camera to capture and preserve the image of Brynn, sitting crosslegged in the straw of the barn floor with Jared in her lap, while the boy cradled a tiny yellow ball of fluff in his pudgy fingers. Sunlight streaming in the door highlighted the gold in her auburn hair and the midnight blue of her eyes. When she bent over Jared, Rand suppressed the urge to lean forward and run his knuckles down the enticing curve of her cheek. Unlike the women he'd dated in the years since his breakup with Sharon, who'd played their sexual attributes to the hilt, Brynn exhibited no awareness of her charms and centered her total attention on Jared.

"Don't squeeze," she warned the boy. "It's just an itty-bitty baby. You don't want to hurt it."

Jared's face filled with awe as the tiny creature moved in his palms. "It's a pwetty itty-bitty."

"Yes, sweetie," she said, hugging him to her. "It is."

At that moment, Rand envied Jared with Brynn's arms around him and her breath tickling his ear.

"The teens take care of the livestock," Gofer was saying. "They feed the chickens, gather eggs, milk the cows and goats, and groom and exercise the horses."

"Sounds like a lot of work," Rand commented but couldn't take his eyes off Brynn.

She lifted her head and curved her lips in a smile that created a hot burst of longing in his stomach. "That's not the half of it. The boys also do all their own cleaning, cooking and laundry, and they plant and maintain the gardens."

"Don't forget their crafts projects," Gofer added.

Rand shook his head. "Talk about hard labor. They're serving a hefty sentence."

"You'd think so," Gofer said, "but the boys love being here."

Rand cast Gofer a skeptical glance. "No offense. Archer Farm's a beautiful spot, but not exactly a teen paradise. No movie theaters, shopping malls or video arcades. And loving all that work…" He shook his head. "I find it hard to believe."

"We screen the boys carefully," Gofer said, "and admit only the ones who are likely to turn their lives around. Once they get here, they find having a purpose and doing a job well are their own rewards, and the positive feedback they receive from the staff fills a void in their lives. We've hit some bumps in the road, but we haven't had to expel a boy yet."

"Let's show him the rest." Brynn shoved to her feet.

"Wanna stay with the chickie," Jared protested.

"We have to let him go back to his mommy," Brynn said softly. "He misses her."

Rand expected more objections, but Jared merely nodded. "Okeedookie."

Gofer led them into a sparkling clean dairy at the side of the barn and introduced Kermit, a black man the size of a small house with a Mr. Universe build, a shaved head and a fierce expression. When he spoke to Jared, however, his dark eyes glowed with kindness and his smile exposed stunning white teeth.

Kermit was supervising four boys, dressed in olive drab pants, shirts and work boots, with white caps covering their hair. Brynn greeted each of the boys by name, and their responses indicated respect and affection for the woman they called Officer Sawyer. Three teens were pasteurizing milk and making goat cheese. One boy was mopping a puddle of milk from the immaculate tile floor beside an overturned pail, the apparent earlier crisis. All the boys worked with quiet efficiency and cooperation. Only the occasional bizarre tattoo flashing on a forearm or rising from the neck of a T-shirt gave any indication of their checkered pasts.

"We sell some of the cheese and milk to Jodie's Café," Kermit explained. "The rest we use here. Five Marines and sixteen teenage boys need a lot of chow."

"We'll leave you to it," Gofer said to Kermit and motioned Rand, Brynn and Jared through an exterior door.

Once the dairy door had closed behind them, Rand said, "Looks like Kermit runs a tight ship."

"We all do," Gofer said. "These boys are hungry for direction and discipline, and they respond well to it."

"Tough love?" Rand asked.

Gofer nodded. "That outburst of profanity you heard earlier will cost Tyrone a hefty fine." He grinned. "We apply it by the word."

"You can't truly appreciate what the staff has done here," Brynn said, "if you didn't see these boys when they arrived. They looked as if they were answering a casting call for a contemporary production of *West Side Story*. The whole gang—and I don't use the word lightly—was one big conglomeration of body piercings, do-rags, hip-hop clothes, snarling faces and attitudes the size of eighteen-wheelers."

She pointed past the dormitory to open fields where several other boys worked. "That's why I say Archer Farm has worked miracles."

"They just needed someone who cares what happens to them," Gofer said.

Lost boys, Rand thought with a long look at Jared. He would do his best to make sure his nephew never joined their ranks. He hoped he could give the boy the love he lacked. Rand's parents had been reserved, showing little physical affection beyond an occasional pat on the head or peck on the cheek. Consequently, he felt ill-equipped to provide Jared the affection he so desperately needed. Despite the differences between their backgrounds, Rand felt a kinship with these boys who'd had so little parental love in their lives.

He observed how Brynn held Jared with an ease he envied. As he watched, she buried her face in the boy's hair and whispered in his ear. Jared smiled and tightened his arms around Brynn's neck. How did she do it? She'd lost her own mother at an early age, but, apparently, the love of an entire town had given her the support she needed to grow into a happy and caring adult.

Rand tore his gaze away and looked over the fields beyond the dorm where another tall, muscular man, a bundle of energy in constant motion, was supervising his charges. One teen drove a John Deere tractor that tilled the red clay soil in preparation for planting. Another was on his knees, setting out lettuce seedlings in cold frames and a third weeded a huge bed of spring flowers.

"That's Ricochet," Gofer said and waved to the man at the far end of the field. "He oversees all the planting."

They turned back toward the huge log building.

"This is the dormitory, both for the boys and the staff," Gofer explained, "except for Jeff, who lives with his wife and stepdaughter in the farmhouse. Brynn helped us build it."

Rand cast her a sideways look. "I'm impressed."

She wrinkled her face in an impish grin. "I'm a woman of many talents."

Rand's contemplation of what her other talents might be made his pulse pound. He pulled hard on the reins of his galloping imagination and followed Gofer up the stairs and into the dorm. He was struck instantly by the mouthwatering aroma of baking mixed with the acrid bite of turpentine.

"Our kitchen." Gofer pointed to the left. "And over here's our living area, commandeered now as a craft center."

In the massive great room, furniture had been pushed against the walls, and tables, made from planks and sawhorses, held a variety of works in progress. One teen, a huge ham-fisted boy, worked supple willow branches into an intricate weave for a basket, while a second teen applied splashes of color to a rustic birdhouse. A stack of finished products included other baskets, decorative wooden plaques and picture frames artistically constructed from twigs.

"Pwetty," Jared said and stretched his hand toward the birdhouse.

"These are beautiful," Brynn said. "Nice work guys!"

"Thanks, Officer Sawyer," one teen said, and both boys grinned with pride at her praise.

In the kitchen, they met Trace, another former Marine, who was in charge of cooking and baking, but held absolutely no resemblance to Betty Crocker. The teens Rand had seen were big kids, but none was as large or as powerfully built as any of the staff who supervised them. Even with a smear of flour across his cheek, Trace looked like a man you wouldn't want to meet in a bar fight or a dark alley. Under his watchful eye, two boys removed cookies and muffins from the oven and transferred the goodies to cooling racks.

"We'll sell these at our booth at Daffodil Days next week," Trace said. "They'll stay fresh in the freezer until then."

"And the crafts?" Rand asked.

"We'll sell them, too," Trace explained. "And bouquets of the flowers we've grown. We're a non-profit organization, so part of the proceeds will go toward the operating costs of the farm and part to the boys themselves. We encourage all our teens to start a savings account for college or vocational school."

"Yeah," one of the boys said with a cocky grin,

"and we all need money for the fine jar, sooner or later."

"You've paid more than your share, Cooper," Gofer said pointedly. "Better keep that in mind."

The boy's expression was the picture of innocence. "But it goes to a good cause, right?"

"A Christmas fund for underprivileged children," Brynn explained to Rand.

Rand's conscience stirred. He'd donated plenty of money to charity in the past, but his giving had been a soulless exercise, prompted more by tax advantages than generosity of spirit. After seeing Archer Farm in operation this morning, he felt a strong desire to help with the work Jeff and his staff were doing. As soon as Rand returned to River Walk, he intended to make a substantial donation, anonymously, to Archer Farm. And while he was at it, he'd write a hefty check for the underprivileged children's Christmas fund, as well.

Chapter Seven

Brynn sat across from Rand at the scrubbed wooden table in the Davidsons' kitchen and found her gaze straying constantly to him. Luckily, Jodie and Jeff were so engrossed in each other, they hadn't noticed Brynn's fascination with their guest of honor, and Rand was preoccupied with Jared.

Jody had served a lunch of homemade chili and cornbread, except to Jared, who'd requested a peanut butter and jelly sandwich. The boy, boosted on his chair by a thick cushion borrowed from the living room sofa, licked grape jelly from his fingers. He turned his face, marked with a milk mustache, to focus intently on whoever was speaking, and just looking at him created a warm, fuzzy feeling beneath Brynn's breastbone.

She wasn't surprised by Jared's effect on her. She'd always loved kids. Having children of her own would be the only reason she'd ever consider giving up police work. When the boy had clasped his chubby arms around her and nuzzled her neck, something soft and tender had broken loose in her heart and slid to her toes. She'd never been particularly interested in marriage, but she'd always wanted a child. But one without the other wasn't an option in her book, so she'd sublimated her desires, spending time as Officer Friendly with schoolchildren and mentoring the Archer Farm boys.

What *had* surprised her was her growing attraction to Rand. She observed him now and realized she could tell a lot about a man from sharing a meal with him. Although he'd just met Jeff and Jodie, he seemed perfectly at ease with their company, praised Jodie's cooking with sincerity and obviously enjoyed his food. His manners were perfect, but not ostentatious, and he held up his end of the conversation with humor and wit.

Brynn suppressed a giggle, recalling a fellow officer from Walhalla with whom she'd ridden on a poker run last year. He'd been impressive to the eye with a handsome face, great physique and his monster Harley, but once they'd stopped for supper at Ridge's Barbecue, she'd been dismayed to discover the man's peculiar obsession. He'd insisted on chewing every mouthful *exactly* thirty-two times before swallowing. The poor guy swore such a process was essential for good digestion. Brynn couldn't imagine enduring another meal with him, much less the thought of spending every morning of her life across the breakfast table from the man.

Rand, on the other hand...

The appeal of that image brought her to a sudden halt, spoon suspended in midair.

"You okay?" Jodie said.

No, she wasn't okay. She was losing her mind. Rand was supposed to be only a diversion, not a man Brynn might consider for the long haul. She barely knew him, for Pete's sake, and what she did know fit with her life about as well as a dress on a cow.

She flashed Jodie a quick smile and hurried to cover for her distraction. "I just remembered I have to work next weekend, so I won't be able to help you at the festival."

"No problem," Jodie said with a glance at Jeff that threatened to melt the man's bones. "Jeff and I have it covered. The boys will help not only at the Archer Farm tables, but at the café, as well. The festival always draws a crowd," she explained to Rand. "Even with so many other food vendors, the café's always crowded."

"After tasting your chili," Rand said, "I'm looking forward to sampling the café's menu."

Jodie flushed with pleasure at his compliment, then turned even redder when Jeff added, "I'm lucky to have a wife who's as great a cook as she is beautiful."

"Must be why I've never married," Brynn cracked. "My idea of cooking is Lean Cuisine and salad in a bag."

"You have lots of talents." Jodie threw the words over her shoulder as she cleared the empty chili bowls from the table.

"Name one," Brynn challenged.

"Target shooting," Jodie replied. "You're a national champion."

"Now that'll make the men come running," Brynn said with a laugh.

"Works for me," Rand said and wiggled his eyebrows.

"See," Jodie exclaimed with a triumphant nod and returned to the table with a tray filled with servings of apple pie and cinnamon ice cream.

"I don't know," Jeff said with a frown as he dug into his dessert. "If I'm ever in the doghouse, I'd rather have a wife with bad aim."

Judging from the sexual tension that had sparked between the newlyweds throughout lunch, Brynn doubted Jeff would find himself in the doghouse any time soon.

"Doggie?" Jared asked and gazed around the room.

Jeff grinned at the child. "We don't have a dog, but I wouldn't mind getting one. Wouldn't mind having a little guy like you, either."

He snagged Jodie around the waist before she sat down and angled a hopeful glance at her.

Jodie rolled her hazel eyes and slid from his embrace. "Sixteen boys aren't enough? Not counting the four overgrown ones you call staff."

"But none of them call me Daddy," Jeff said.

Jodie's expression softened at those words. "We might be able to negotiate something."

With a look hot enough to raise steam, Jeff batted her playfully on her upper arm. "Negotiating's the best part."

"Jeff Davidson, will you behave?" Jodie shook her head in feigned exasperation, but Brynn could tell she loved Jeff's teasing.

Brynn cast a look at Rand, who was watching the newlyweds with an amused expression, and wondered what he was thinking. She also found herself wondering why he'd never married and had children of his own. He had to be several years older than her. Brynn figured he was probably as married to his work as she was.

"Brynn," Jodie said, breaking her train of thought, "if you see your aunt Marion or uncle Bud before I have a chance to call them, tell them I want to rent the upstairs over the café." She turned to Rand. "My daughter Brittany and I lived there before Jeff and I were married. It will make someone a nice apartment, or even office space."

"I'm sorry I didn't have a chance to meet Brittany," Rand said, and hastily reached to grab Jared's spoon before the child dropped a dollop of melting ice cream onto the floor.

"She's working at the café today," Jodie said with a sigh, "which is probably just as well. At fifteen, she doesn't have much use for grown-ups. We, as she would say, are *so* out of it."

"I have the teen years to look forward to," Rand said with a glance at Jared, "if I survive childhood. I'm learning as I go."

"All parents do," Jodie said with a knowing grin, "and when you finally get the hang of it, the kids have grown up and move out."

And then they're gone. The line of a country music hit from a few years back popped into Brynn's head. But she wasn't thinking of grown children leaving home. She was contemplating Rand and Jared's return to New York, and the prospect made her chest ache.

She stifled a curse. Look what she'd gone and done. Not only was she falling hard for a man who was her polar opposite, his adorable nephew had tangled himself in her heartstrings, as well. And soon both would return to New York. So much for her superficial spring fling. She'd flung herself, all right. Right into a whole heap of heartbreak trouble.

"You on a diet?" Jodie asked.

"What?" Brynn shook off her reverie.

"You haven't touched your pie." Jodie pointed to Brynn's full plate.

Brynn forced a smile and picked up her fork. "Just savoring the anticipation."

She took a mouthful of the sweet concoction, aware every second of Jodie's scrutiny. Jodie, along with Merrilee, was Brynn's best friend in the whole world, and Brynn would have to be very careful. She knew from experience, she couldn't hide anything from either one of them. And if Jodie and Merrilee caught even a whiff of Brynn's attraction to Rand, Brynn would never hear the end of it.

AN HOUR LATER, Rand was maneuvering the Jaguar smoothly around the switchbacks down the mountain, Jared was asleep in his carrier and Brynn sat in the passenger seat, every nerve ending humming with awareness of the man beside her. With the radio off and the quietness of the expensive engine, she could hear him breathe, an intimate, comforting sound.

"Your friends are good people," Rand said, breaking the silence. "And they're doing terrific work with those teens. I have to admit, I was skeptical when you suggested this visit, but now I'm really glad I went."

"Archer Farm is a unique place," Brynn said.

Her mind, however, wasn't on the farm or the teens. All she could think of was how much she was attracted to Rand, from his thick brown, professionally styled hair to the tips of his expensive Gucci loafers. And especially everything in between. For someone with his obvious fortune and prestigious career, he'd acted remarkably at home in the Davidsons' cheery kitchen and had related easily to his hosts, just like a regular guy. She wondered if he pre-

ferred champagne to beer, whether he ever watched
football games on Sunday afternoons, or got his
well-manicured hands dirty working around the
house or in the yard. And the million dollar question:
would he be here long enough for her to find out?

Her gut warned her to cut her losses and run, to
avoid any further contact with Rand and Jared so
their eventual departure wouldn't hurt. But her heart
was a different story.

"It's been such a great day—" Rand slanted her
a look that made her suddenly hot in her bulky
sweater "—that I don't want it to end. Come back
to River Walk with us. You haven't had a chance to
see the place in daylight."

No way, her mind was screaming, but her reply
came her heart. "I'd love to."

His face lit up like Fourth of July fireworks, his delight so obvious Brynn had to look away. She restrained
herself from beating her head against the passenger
window in frustration. Why hadn't she just said no?

*Because Rand Benedict is a very special man,
maybe the one you've been looking for all your life,*
a voice inside her head insisted.

But she hadn't been looking for a man, not even
a special one. Had she?

Certainly not one who would pull up stakes, head
north into Yankee land and take her heart with him.
And the harder she tried to maintain that he was still

a lowdown skunk of a lawyer, the more Rand did to disprove her bias.

His parting words to Jeff had been a good example. In the gravel parking lot, Rand had pulled a thin leather folder from his shirt pocket, extracted a card and handed it to Jeff. "I'd like to help out here. If you ever need legal assistance of any kind, give me a call."

Jeff had thrown a calculating glance at the sleek Jag and shook his head. "I'm afraid Archer Farm can't afford your fees."

"Who said anything about paying?" Rand had said with steel in his voice. "Anything you need, I'll provide pro bono. It's the least I can do."

Just remembering his offer made Brynn want to unhook her seat belt and hug Rand breathless.

As if tuned to her thoughts, he reached across the console between the seats, took her hand and laced his fingers through hers. His skin was warm, his grip strong and she didn't have the will to pull away.

"Didn't you ever take a defensive driving course?" she asked.

He shook his head. "Why?"

"You'd have learned to keep both hands on the wheel."

He lifted her hand, still clasped in his. "Your objection personal or professional?"

Tell him it's personal, her head insisted, but her heart prevailed. "Professional. I'm a stickler for rules."

He laughed with a deep rich chuckle that warmed her bones. "We make a good pair, you and me."

She cast him a glance, her lips quirked in skepticism. "Right. We have *so* much in common."

"Don't you see? We're like the TV show. *Law and Order,* that's us."

Us. The word pulled at her with possibilities, then punished her with problems.

"Funny," she said, struggling for levity. "I never thought of myself as looking like Jerry Orbach."

He laughed again and released her hand to make the turn toward River Walk.

Lillian must have heard the car's approach, because the housekeeper was waiting when they pulled in front of the house. Noting that Jared was asleep, she merely waved in greeting, then lifted the boy from his carrier and took him inside to complete his nap.

Brynn stepped out of the car into the warm spring air, shucked her sweater over her head and tossed it on the front seat. Shrugging out of his leather jacket, Rand circled the car.

"Ever taken the river walk the house is named for?" he asked.

Brynn shook her head, gazed first at his loafers, then at her own high-heeled boots. "We're not exactly dressed for hiking."

"We won't be blazing a trail, just following a carefully constructed one."

He held out his hand. She placed hers in his and allowed him to lead her across the main deck toward the rear of the house and down a series of stairs. At the river's edge, they stepped onto a path, constructed of pea gravel and lined with heavy timbers, that meandered with the river. In summer, overhanging branches of poplar, maples and oaks would form a shady canopy, but today the bud-laden branches merely threw a lacy twig pattern across the path. Scattered at random on either side of the walkway, as if sown by nature instead of man, were plantings of bright yellow forsythia, white jonquils, pink and lavender tulips and deep purple irises.

"I had no idea this was here," Brynn said. "It's a linear garden."

"The original owner had it planted for his wife, who loved flowers. The real estate agent assured me there are flowers for every season, from now through fall, especially roses. And evergreens, too—" he pointed to nandina and hollies "—for winter color."

"Too bad you won't be here to enjoy it all." Brynn withdrew her hand from his at the reminder of his coming departure.

"I'll be here awhile."

"Till summer?"

"I'm not sure." He avoided her gaze by looking out over the river tumbling below them at the bottom of the bank. "But this is our vacation home, so we'll be back often."

Hope blossomed, but only for an instant before withering again. "You've admitted you're a workaholic. How often do you take vacations?"

He reached down and plucked a deep pink tulip and handed it to her. "I'm taking one now."

"And how long since your last one?"

"I went skiing in Tahoe a little over a year ago."

"Let me guess. You went with clients. You were working on a deal."

His eyes widened in alarm. "How do you know that?"

"From everything I've observed about you. You never relax, not without a purpose."

He placed his hands on her shoulders and turned her to face him. "I'm relaxed now."

His breath, still faint with cinnamon from Jodie's ice cream, caressed her face. Above them, a crab apple, its gnarled branches thick with lacy blossoms, blocked the sun.

"Don't look at me like that," she warned.

"Like what?"

"Like a long-time dieter contemplating a hot-fudge sundae."

Desire swirled in the brown depths of his eyes, and a corresponding wave of heat rolled through her stomach.

"Why, Officer Sawyer, I didn't know you'd been holding out on me."

"What?" Longing fogged her brain.

"You never told me you could read minds."

Before she could respond, he dipped his head, pulled her to him and claimed her lips with his. Her body seemed to soften and transform, like a shape-shifter's, molding to him with the fluid quality of liquid mercury. She lifted her arms around his neck, and he slid his hands around her waist and pressed her closer.

She wanted to consume him, to be devoured by him, to blur the lines where Rand began and she ended. She opened herself to his kiss, and their tongues touched, breaths mingled. His pulse vibrated through the rock-hardness of his muscles, and the beat of his heart speeded and synchronized with hers. She threaded her fingers through the silky thickness of his hair, while his hands massaged her back in mind-blowing circles.

The backfire of a truck echoed from the distant highway and brought her to her senses. She pulled away, gasping for breath, like a diver breaking the surface after a too-deep plunge. She tugged at the hem of her blouse, more to still her trembling fingers than from a need to straighten it.

Rand kept his arms around her waist, and she leaned back to gaze at him.

His remarkable mouth that had just driven her to the edge of wildness curved in a slow grin. "Know what you taste like?" he asked.

"Cinnamon?" she guessed.

He shook his head. "You taste like *more*."

"More what?" Brynn asked.

"More kisses." His words were teasing, but his eyes were serious.

His kiss had shattered her reason, broken through her reserves and blown her innate caution to the four winds. The last thing she needed now was what she wanted most: to kiss him again.

She placed her hands against the broad expanse of his chest and pushed herself from the temptation. "We shouldn't go there."

Disappointment wreathed his face. "You didn't like it?"

"I liked it too much. But why travel down a dead-end road?"

His features relaxed at her admission of enjoyment. "Carpe diem?"

"Seize the day?" She didn't know whether she was angry with herself, him, the circumstances or all of the above. "You want short-term thrills, take a trip to Dollywood."

He puckered his features in confusion. "Dollywood?"

She heaved a sigh of exasperation. "Dolly Parton's theme park in Pigeon Forge, Tennessee. Don't you Yankees know anything?"

With that parting shot, she pivoted on her heel and started back toward the house, not trusting herself to be alone with Rand a minute longer.

Chapter Eight

Spurred by a sense of eager anticipation, Rand parked his silver Jag in the crowded lot of the First Baptist Church on Saturday morning. He'd been to other flea markets—bigger events than this one, like the outdoor sales in Little Italy in New York—but never had he felt like a kid on his way to a candy store.

As he climbed out of his car and locked it, part of the reason was obvious. Brynn was working, so he was sure to run into her patrolling the activities of Daffodil Days. He'd phoned often since last Saturday, but she hadn't returned his calls. After he'd kissed her at River Walk last week, she'd been polite, but standoffish, and had thanked him primly for a nice day when he'd delivered her to her door. But her coolness had contrasted sharply with the fire he'd felt when he'd held her, and she continued to draw him like a flame lures a moth.

He wouldn't apologize for kissing her. How could

he say he was sorry for something he'd enjoyed so much that he couldn't get it out of his mind? But maybe he could melt her chilly attitude and convince her to spend time with him again.

He circled the barricade that blocked all but pedestrian traffic from the main street and stepped into the crowd. His gaze swept the tables and booths assembled along the curbs, and he was jolted with a second reason for his anticipation of the day. He *liked* these people and their little town. In Pleasant Valley, he'd encountered a sense of belonging that he'd never experienced before, certainly not in the rarefied atmosphere of the Hamptons where he'd grown up, nor in the dog-eat-dog jungle of corporate law.

Hoping to run into Brynn, Rand had come into town often during the past week. He'd shopped for Lillian at Blalock's Grocery, walked the aisles of Fulton's Department Store and bought a soda and a moon pie—the latter confection recommended by the clerk—at Paulie's Drugstore. Everyone he'd met had been friendly and welcoming, offering gracious and attentive service and pleasant conversation, the likes of which he seldom received in his home city. But his quest to run into Brynn had proved futile, and he hoped for better luck today.

Above the hubbub of voices and music, a familiar voice called his name. Rand turned to see Jodie, manning a table outside the café. He threaded his way through the crowd and bought a cup of coffee from her. In spite of being harried with sales, she flashed him a warm smile and took time to inquire after Jared.

At the next table, Gofer sat with three of the boys from Archer Farm, doing a brisk business as buyers scooped up items from their display of crafts. *Like ducks on a June bug,* Rand thought with a smile, remembering the colorful turn of phrase from a story Tom Fulton had shared with Rand in his store. When Gofer glimpsed Rand, his face split in a cordial grin.

The next vendor Rand spotted was Vera Mauney, Joe's wife, seated beneath one of the spreading maples that lined the street, with an array of buckets and pails spread out at her feet. Each vessel was filled with water and packed tight with bouquets of spring flowers, including the ubiquitous cheery daffodils for which the festival was named. Vera caught his eye, smiled and waved.

Rand waved back and recalled his meeting with the Mauneys a few days ago. Farrington had been pushing Rand for results, so he'd visited the Mauney farm, after phoning to ask if he could bring Jared to see the cows. Vera's response had been immediate and enthusiastic. "Come and stay for lunch. We're always happy to see our neighbors."

Her unbridled hospitality had stung his conscience, since his intent hadn't been so much a social call as a scheme to scope out the Mauney property before making an offer for Farrington to purchase it.

Vera's husband Joe, a big man of few words and a face weathered by age and the elements, had escorted Rand and Jared around the meticulously maintained dairy barn with its shining stainless steel milking machines. Then they had strolled over the gently rolling fields, gloriously lush and green with the first growth of spring under the bright April sun. The dairyman hadn't needed words to express the pride he took in his work or the love he had for his land. As he walked his farm, his face displayed the same emotions that a man might feel for his new bride or his firstborn.

The way Rand was beginning to feel about Brynn....

"That oak—" Joe pointed to a massive tree that would shade the entire farmhouse once its branches leafed out, "—has been here over three hundred years. That's why my great-great-granddaddy chose this spot to build this house in 1768. Been Mauneys living here ever since. Always will be."

It was the longest speech Joe had made that day.

At lunch in the sunny country kitchen, Rand had met Joe's son, Josh, another huge man who said little but whose eyes also shone with pride when he spoke of the Mauney farm.

"You have a lot of valuable property here," Rand had remarked casually. "After buying River Walk, I know how high land values are. You ever thought of selling and retiring?"

The entire family had frozen at his words, as if he'd suggested they cut off their right arms. Joe finally shook his head. "Some things you can't put a price on," he said before taking another bite of Vera's succulent chicken casserole and dropping the subject.

Rand had left with a hand-carved wooden whistle Joe had given Jared and a huge jar of pear preserves put up by Vera. Rand also carried away the conviction that the Mauneys would never sell, that Farrington Properties could never acquire Mauney's acres, no matter how much they offered. But Rand had consoled himself, knowing he still had a shot at Eileen Bickerstaff's farm.

Several yards ahead on the street through the press of people, he spotted Brynn in front of a table. The lines of her tailored uniform and her officer's cap made her appear taller than he remembered, but the austere cut of the navy shirt and slacks did nothing to camouflage the perfection of her sweet curves. And the shadow of her hat couldn't hide the flawless bones of her face, or her eyes, a deep-water blue a man could drown in, or the saucy grin that reminded him of the taste of her kiss.

The grin, unfortunately, wasn't aimed at him. She was talking directly to an ancient, stately woman who sat behind a table of glistening jars of jellies and jams and bottles of sparkling wine, but he could sense Brynn's general alertness. On duty, she was aware of everyone and everything around her, and, he realized with a sinking heart, she had noticed him, too, but refused to acknowledge his presence.

He hurried to catch her before she moved on. "Good morning, Brynn."

She turned, hands on her hips, and tilted her head up to meet his gaze. Sunlight, and a fleeting emotion he couldn't identify, sparked in her eyes. "Hi, Rand. Where's Jared?"

"Home with Lillian. I thought I'd check things out this morning and bring him back this afternoon for a shorter stay."

Brynn nodded toward a table in front of the Hair Apparent. "Amy Lou's doing face paintings for kids. And there's a merry-go-round set up on the school grounds. Jared might get a kick out of those."

"Thanks. You working all day?" He hoped to talk her into dinner or at least a drink later.

Her relief was painfully evident when she answered, "The whole department's on overtime for the duration of the festival."

Rand, however, wasn't about to give up. "When's your next time off?"

A strong female voice with a hint of gravel in its tone interrupted. "Brynn, aren't you going to introduce me to your young man?"

A flush of deep color worked it way from the collar of Brynn's uniform to her cheeks. "Sure, Mrs.

Bickerstaff. This is Rand Benedict. He lives at River Walk. And he's not *my* young man."

The woman stood behind the table and stretched her hand across. "Howdy-do, Rand. Guess you can say we're neighbors, although I do live up the road a piece."

Rand tore his gaze from Brynn and shook Mrs. Bickerstaff's hand. The woman was almost as tall as he was, with a ramrod posture and unexpectedly regal bearing at ninety-six. Her white hair was arranged in a style reminiscent of pictures of Gibson Girls and framed a face remarkably unlined. Soft gray eyes twinkled with a youthful spirit behind silver-rimmed glasses. Rand guessed she must have been a real beauty when she was younger.

"You're the blackberry lady," he said.

Mrs. Bickerstaff laughed. "I've been called worse. And you're the Yankee lawyer."

"I've been called worse," Rand admitted with a grin, warming to the old woman.

"If you'll excuse me," Brynn said to her, "I have work to do."

"Wait!" Mrs. Bickerstaff stated aloud what Rand's heart was shouting. "I have a favor to ask, Brynn, although I really shouldn't, considering how much you do for me already."

Brynn's smile for the woman was filled with affection and made Rand wish she'd look at him that way. "Anything you need, Mrs. Bickerstaff. I'm happy to help."

"It involves your young man here."

Brynn smile vanished. "He's not my young man."

Mrs. Bickerstaff flicked an age-spotted hand, dismissing Brynn's objection. "I want you to bring him out to my house next week."

"What?" Brynn's mouth dropped open.

Rand blinked in surprise. This was his lucky day. The two things he wanted most, being with Brynn and checking out Blackberry Farm, had dropped into his lap like a present from the blue.

Mrs. Bickerstaff turned to him. "You don't mind, do you?"

"I'd be happy to visit you."

"But—" Brynn sputtered.

"It's not a social call," the old woman said. "It's business."

"Business?" Rand's mind whirled. Had the shrewd old woman gotten wind of his purpose? Was she willing to sell? Was she actually going to make his job that easy? Her next words took the wind from his sails.

"I need you to draw up my will."

"Your will?" Brynn had finally found her voice. "You don't have a will, Mrs. Bickerstaff?"

"Of course I do. Anyone my age would be a fool not to. But I want mine changed. And the sooner the better."

"You're not ill?" Brynn's concerned gaze raked the woman's face.

"Fit as a fiddle," Mrs. Bickerstaff said, "but at

ninety-six, I don't have time to dally. And I don't want to travel all the way to that attorney in Walhalla for a new will. If you'd take care of it, Rand, I'd be most grateful."

"He's from New York," Brynn said. "He can't practice law in South Carolina."

"Ah, but he can," Mrs. Bickerstaff said with a smile. "I've done my homework. Mr. Benedict's firm has an office in Charleston, as well as Denver and Miami. He's licensed to practice here, as well as in New York, Colorado and Florida."

"But you don't need me," Brynn protested.

"Oh, but I do," she replied earnestly. "If you come on Monday, Caroline Tuttle will be there. That's the day she helps with the housecleaning. You two can be witnesses."

"So it's a simple will?" Rand asked.

Mrs. Bickerstaff shook her head. "Actually, it's quite complicated. That's why I need a good lawyer. And why I've looked up your credentials, young man. You'll do."

He knotted his eyebrows in question, wondering *how* she'd checked him out.

The old woman must have noted his puzzlement. "I may live in an isolated part of the valley," she said, "but I can surf with the best of 'em. Ever looked yourself up on the Web?"

"No," Rand said.

"Ought to try it sometime."

"I'd be honored to help with your will." Rand would have agreed to mucking out her barn if it meant spending time with Brynn, who was watching the conversation like a spectator at a tennis match, but making no comment. His only reservation was that he'd have to come clean with Mrs. Bickerstaff about his firm's client wanting to buy her land before Rand helped with her will, so there would be no question of a conflict of interest.

"Good, it's settled then." Mrs. Bickerstaff rubbed her arthritic hands together. "If you come in the afternoon, you and Brynn can stay for supper."

Rand noted that a variety of emotions scudded across Brynn's face like storm clouds before resignation settled in.

"I'll pick you up at two o'clock Monday afternoon," Brynn said to him. "Now, if you'll both excuse me, I have a job to do."

She turned on her heel and waded through the crowd. Rand watched her go.

"Brynn's a lovely girl," Mrs. Bickerstaff said.

"Yes, she is."

"And she likes you."

Rand felt as if he'd been handed another gift. "You think so? Seemed like she couldn't get away from me fast enough."

Mrs. Bickerstaff laughed, exposing perfect white teeth. "That's one of the ways I know she likes you."

Rand shook his head. "You could be wrong…."

"I've known Brynn since she was a baby, and I can read her like a book. She likes you, but she's trying her darnedest not to let it show."

"Well, she's doing a good job."

Mrs. Bickerstaff winked with a sly nod. "Don't let her scare you off."

"I'm more worried about the other way around," Rand admitted. "She thinks we have nothing in common."

"Hmmmpht. Brynn's a smart girl, but she doesn't know everything. You keep after her, you hear?"

Rand laughed. "What are you, Pleasant Valley's *shadchen?*"

Her white eyebrows drew together in a frown. "I don't know that word."

"It's Yiddish for matchmaker."

Mrs. Bickerstaff's smile returned. "I've been called worse," she said with another wink.

"I'll see you Monday," Rand said and walked away.

He spent the rest of the morning wandering through the streets, admiring the arts and crafts, examining some amazing antiques and sampling alien delicacies such as sourwood honey on fresh-baked biscuits and peanut-butter candy, an unlikely confection of powdered sugar, peanut butter and mashed potatoes.

That afternoon, he returned with Jared, who squealed with joy on the merry-go-round and sat stoically while Amy Lou Baker painted a daffodil on his cheek. Jared also consumed the peanut butter candy as if he hadn't eaten in a week. Rand caught sight of Brynn often in the crowd, but she was always at a distance, so he didn't have a chance to speak with her again.

MONDAY AFTERNOON, Brynn sat in Eileen Bickerstaff's kitchen and watched Caroline Tuttle scrub the ancient stove where Eileen cooked her blackberry delicacies. She could hear the murmur of voices up the hall behind the closed doors of the parlor, but she couldn't discern what Rand and Mrs. Bickerstaff were saying. Whatever they were discussing was taking a long time.

Brynn wasn't interested in the woman's last will and testament, but she'd caught the matchmaking gleam in the old woman's eyes when Eileen had first met Rand. Bad enough that Aunt Marion was trying to drag Brynn to the altar. Her aunt didn't need help from Mrs. Bickerstaff.

A teakettle on the back burner whistled. Caroline, who was only a couple years older than Brynn, turned off the stove and poured the boiling water into a teapot. "Want a cup?" she asked Brynn.

"Sure," Brynn said. "Looks like you could use a break. Don't you get enough housekeeping at your place?"

Agnes Tuttle, Caroline's hypochondriac mother,

might own a bed-and-breakfast, the only lodgings in town, but *Caroline* did all the work.

Caroline shrugged and took cups and saucers of fine bone china from a cabinet by the sink. "I enjoy getting away from home, even if it's only twice a month. And Mrs. Bickerstaff is a pleasure to work for."

Unlike Caroline's mother.

The unspoken words hung in the air between them. Everyone in town knew Agnes used her myriad ailments as an excuse to keep Caroline under her thumb. The devoted daughter seemed doomed to a life of fetching and carrying, because the B and B kept her too busy to meet new people, except for the inn's guests, who were merely passing through. Rumor had it that Caroline had been sweet on Grant Nathan, the vet, but he'd married Merrilee Stratton last year. If Caroline was nursing a broken heart, it didn't show. Women in town had always envied Caroline's Princess Diana good looks and had shaken their heads over the fact that some lucky man hadn't stolen her from Agnes's clutches.

Looking elegant, even in jeans and a sweatshirt with a blue bandanna holding back her ash-blond hair, Caroline poured the tea, set a cup in front of Brynn, then sat opposite her at the round farm table of well-scrubbed oak.

"You doing okay?" Brynn asked.

Caroline looked over her teacup in surprise. "I'm good. Why shouldn't I be?"

Brynn shrugged. "I don't know. I thought, what with Grant marrying Merrilee—"

"Pshaw," Caroline said. "I was never interested in Grant."

"You weren't?" Brynn raised her eyebrows in surprise.

"Not for years, since I dated Grant in high school. But my mother thought I should be. She started the rumors, hoping something would come of them." Caroline rolled her eyes. "Mother relished the idea of a veterinary doctor for a son-in-law."

Brynn shook her head and grinned. "She probably told Amy Lou, who spread the word like jungle drums."

"Speaking of rumors—" Caroline cocked her head toward the parlor "—plenty are circling about you and the Yankee lawyer. After meeting him, I hope, for your sake, they're true."

"You know how people talk," Brynn said hastily, "but it's only talk."

"Too bad," Caroline said. "He's the best-looking thing to hit town since Jeff Davidson and his Marines landed."

"But he won't be here long," Brynn insisted, as much to herself as to Caroline. "He bought River Walk as a vacation home, but I wouldn't be surprised if he doesn't keep it. He's not the type to take vacations."

"Like you?" Caroline said with a smile.

"And you," Brynn said.

"Touché. But I can't leave Mother alone with her health the way it is."

Brynn bit her tongue. Agnes Tuttle, she thought with a burst of anger at Caroline's plight, would outlive them all. She was too damned mean to die. How such a woman and her long-dead henpecked husband had produced a daughter as sweet and lovely as Caroline was one of God's great mysteries.

The pocket doors of the parlor rattled open, and Rand and Eileen came down the hall into the kitchen. Brynn grabbed her teacup with both hands and gazed into its depths to avoid staring at Rand. She didn't want to admit, even to herself, how much she liked the sight of him.

When she'd left her house earlier in the afternoon to pick him up at River Walk, she'd found herself giddy with the prospect of seeing him again, like a teenage girl waiting for her first prom date. When she'd parked in front of the house and climbed out of her car, it had been Jared, not Rand, who'd greeted her.

The front door had flown open, and the toddler had rushed down the steps and flung his arms around her knees, almost knocking her off balance in his enthusiasm.

"Bwynn! Where you been? I missed you."

She leaned down and swooped him into her arms. "I missed you, too, sweetie."

Jared planted a wet kiss on her cheek, and Brynn buried her face in his hair. His arms tightened around her neck. "Ossifer Fwienly missed you, too."

Brynn drew back to see his face. "Have you met any little boys or girls to play with?"

Jared shook his head. "Just Lillian."

Brynn glanced up. Rand stood in the doorway, watching them with a peculiar look on his face. In spite of her determination to remain aloof from his charms, her pulse raced at the sight of him.

"You ready?" she asked.

He nodded. "Jared, you have to stay with Lillian."

The boy's lower lip trembled. "Wanna go wif Bwynn."

"Not this time, sweetie. Your Uncle Rand has work to do."

"Play wif me?" Jared begged, his tone more pitiful than petulant.

Over his head, her gaze met Rand's with dismay. She hated disappointing the lonely little boy.

"Brynn will play with you when we come back," Rand promised.

"We're staying for supper at Blackberry Farm," Brynn reminded him. "It'll be late."

"Staying up this once won't hurt him," Rand said.

Brynn, torn between her pull toward Jared and her intentions to distance herself from Rand, hesitated. The little boy was lonely and needed a friend. But being alone in the house with Rand, even with Lillian close by... If Rand tried to kiss her again, Brynn wasn't sure she could resist.

Jared reached up and placed his hands on her cheeks. "Pwease?"

Always a sucker for kids and animals, Brynn gave in. "Okay, sweetie, I'll see you after supper."

Lillian came out and took the boy. Rand, carrying his laptop in a case slung over his shoulder, hopped into the passenger seat, and Brynn slid behind the wheel.

Although the drive had taken less than ten minutes, Brynn's superawareness of Rand beside her had made it seem like forever. Why did he have to look and smell so good?

"Jared needs friends his own age," she said, hoping a neutral subject would break the tension that hung between them.

Rand chuckled. "Back to blunt again?"

She kept her eyes on the road, but she could feel his smile. "The Community Church has a Mother's Morning Out twice a week. Playing with the children there would be good for Jared."

"That's a thought."

His answer made her frown. "Of course, if you won't be here much longer..."

She waited, wondering what he'd say, half of her hoping he'd announce an imminent departure to end her exquisite torture, the other half longing for him to stay.

"I'll discuss it with Lillian," he said.

"Fine." So much for her interrogation skills. Maybe she could weasel more information from him after supper.

After arriving at Blackberry Farm, Rand had joined Eileen in the front parlor, and Brynn had gone into the kitchen to wait.

Drawing up the will had taken longer than Brynn had expected, even though Rand had his computer and Eileen had hers and her printer set up in the parlor.

With the ordeal completed, Eileen sank into a chair beside Brynn and waved Rand into another. "I'll have some of that tea, please, Caroline. All this legal mumbo-jumbo has taken the starch out of me."

Caroline poured tea for both of them and returned to her seat. Rand shuffled an impressive stack of printed pages in front of him and drew a Mont Blanc pen from the pocket of his shirt.

"All I need now," he said, "are signatures. Mrs. Bickerstaff, you sign first, and initial each page. Then Brynn and Caroline can witness."

After the women had signed, Rand handed one copy to Eileen and slid the other into his computer case.

Caroline stood to leave. "Mother expects her supper on time. I'd better hurry."

She kissed Mrs. Bickerstaff's cheek and left through the back door. The sound of her car's engine and its wheels on the gravel carried into the kitchen.

Mrs. Bickerstaff pulled a ceramic cookie jar from a cabinet over the refrigerator, stuffed her copy of the will inside, and returned the container to the shelf. "Your young man knows his stuff."

Brynn bit back a correction. Eileen was apparently determined to think of Rand as Brynn's young man, and protests were futile.

"Wills are fairly standard," Rand said. "I just filled in the blanks. But I was happy to help."

Eileen glanced at the clock. "Lordy me, look at the time. I promised y'all supper, so I'd better get these old bones moving."

SINCE MEETING Brynn, a seed had taken root in Rand's mind, and every new encounter with her and the people of Pleasant Valley nourished it. In Eileen Bickerstaff's homey kitchen, dining on country ham, collard greens and pinto beans, Rand felt his idea blossom and flourish.

After completing Eileen's will, Rand knew without doubt that she had no intention of selling Blackberry Farm to Farrington Properties or anyone else. Her plans for the future of her longtime home were definite and immutable. And fascinating. Rand hoped the woman had many more good years, but he also hoped to be around to see her incredible scheme implemented. For now, however, under the cloak of attorney-client privilege, her exceptional secret was safe with him.

Mrs. Bickerstaff's refusal to sell meant his quest for Farrington Properties had failed, which also meant his senior partnership at Steinman, Slagle and Crump was toast. But, amazingly, he really didn't care. Finishing off his meal with a bowl of Eileen's exceptional blackberry cobbler, Rand felt nothing but contentment, a state he'd experienced far too seldom in the past and looked forward to enjoying more.

The main reason for his happiness was Brynn, whom he intended to spend as much time with as he could. And a secondary but significant influence on his contentment was the community that had produced this remarkable woman. For the first time in his life, Rand had found a place where he felt he belonged, not just some stopping off point to somewhere else. Not that New York wasn't a great city. It was the best. And filled with plenty of good people, too. The problem was the kind of life he'd chosen when he'd lived there. Now he'd changed. He was ready to put down roots.

Doing Eileen's will had given him the final push toward his decision. Pleasant Valley didn't have a law practice, and the space over Jodie's café would make a perfect spot for him to set up shop. With the money he'd accumulated over the years, he didn't have to worry about an income. Even if all he did was pro bono work, he had more than enough financial security for him and Jared.

And Brynn.

A slight crack appeared in his contentment. Would he be able to convince her to share a life with him here in the valley? He knew she was attracted to him. He'd felt her response when he'd kissed her. But he knew, too, that she was fighting her feelings. She'd avoided his eyes all through supper and had aimed most of her remarks at Mrs. Bickerstaff.

He'd have to tread carefully, win her over gradually. As much as he longed to tell her his plans, he'd wait until the moment was right. Even if it took weeks. Months. After all, now that he'd made his decision to remain in Pleasant Valley, he had all the time in the world.

Chapter Nine

The sun was setting when Rand and Brynn returned to River Walk. Explaining that she was accustomed to turning in at eight, Mrs. Bickerstaff had served an early supper. Jared would be waiting up for them, and Rand found the boy's insistence that Brynn come back to play with him another reason in Rand's long list of why he loved the child. If Rand was lucky, Lillian would retire to the guest house in time to watch *Wheel of Fortune* and *Jeopardy,* and he would have Brynn all to himself.

Brynn parked her SUV in front of the main steps and turned to him. "It was kind of you to help Mrs. Bickerstaff."

"She's an interesting lady." Rand picked up his laptop from the car floor. "Knows more about the world through her computer than a lot of international travelers."

Brynn unhooked her seat belt. "Living alone, she finds the Web a good companion."

"What did she do before the Internet?"

"Worked like an ox. She still has a milk cow and a kitchen garden and her blackberries, but when she was younger, she picked the fruit from her orchards and raised her own crops for market."

"All that activity must be what keeps her healthy."

Brynn shook her head and opened the car door. "She attributes her longevity to her daily glass of blackberry wine."

Rand climbed from the car, slung the strap of his laptop carrier over his shoulder, and joined Brynn on the steps.

"I have a confession," he said.

She angled her head and looked up at him. The last rays of sunlight glinted in her hair and reflected in the depths of her eyes, and her expression was a mixture of curiosity and concern. "Should I read you your Miranda rights?"

He smiled and shook his head. "I haven't committed a crime, but it still doesn't feel right. Mrs. Bickerstaff insisted on paying me."

Brynn relaxed at his admission. "She would. She's a very proud and self-reliant woman."

"But she insisted on paying me my standard rate," Rand said with a frown. "Said she'd checked with my office."

"Whoa," Brynn laughed. "That *is* a crime. I believe they call it highway robbery."

"I protested, but she wouldn't budge. Said she

didn't want special treatment, that I'd earned every penny, especially by making a house call."

"If the new will sets her mind at ease, you've done her a favor," Brynn said.

"What, no lawyer jokes to cover a situation like this?"

"Lawyer jokes?" Brynn asked with a delightful blush. "Who ratted me out?"

"Eileen." He shoved his hands deep in his pockets to keep from reaching for her.

"My co-conspirator," Brynn sighed. "You can blame her for aiding and abetting. She's always e-mailing new jokes she picks up on the Web."

"No problem." Rand shrugged, not taking her choice of humor personally. "Lawyer bashing is as American as apple pie."

Brynn nodded. "I suppose everyone knows at least one lawyer joke."

"And for every good lawyer joke," Rand admitted, "there's probably at least one bad lawyer."

Her gaze caught his and her expression sobered. "I'm learning you're not one of them."

The warmth in her eyes caused a hitch in his breathing. He knew what she meant, but he wanted to hear her say it. "Not a lawyer?"

"Not a bad lawyer. You've really been great, offering to help with Archer Farm's legal work, doing Mrs. Bickerstaff's will."

Her admission flooded him with a satisfying feeling of accomplishment no deal for Steinman, Slagle and Crump had ever provided. "But I'm still a Yankee."

Brynn grimaced. "Eileen told you about the Yankee jokes, too?"

The old woman had proved a fount of information. "Mrs. Bickerstaff told me everything about you."

Brynn shook her head. "She's worse than my aunt Marion."

Unable to resist another second, Rand grasped her by the shoulders and searched her face. "You say I'm not a bad lawyer. Am I a bad Yankee?"

Her eyes twinkled with mischief. "Is there any other kind?"

"Ouch, that hurts."

Her expression sobered, and she placed her hand over his heart. "Sorry. In your case, maybe I'm willing to make an exception."

"An exception?" He wanted to kiss her so much, he could taste her, and her floral scent was driving him crazy with need.

Her teasing grin returned. "I'm willing to be lenient and call you simply geographically challenged."

He placed his hand over hers and pressed it against his chest, ready to pull her close and claim her lips.

Jared's voice interrupted. "Bwynn! You comed to play wif me!"

Squealing with delight, he slipped out the front door and bounded down the steps. In his excitement, he stumbled and would have fallen if Brynn, with lightning-fast reflexes, hadn't whirled and scooped him up.

"I promised I would, sweetie. And I never break a promise."

Rand savored the scene of Brynn with Jared in her arms, their faces close, eyes shining. He could get used to a sight like that, a picture that filled him with contentment and an unaccustomed sense of peace—

Which Lillian immediately shattered when she followed Jared down the steps. "Charles Steinman called this afternoon, Mr. Benedict. Said his message is urgent. He insists you call him at the office first thing in the morning."

"Thanks, Lillian." Rand would call Steinman tomorrow, but not with the news his high-powered boss wanted to hear. Not only would Rand concede defeat at obtaining the acreage Farrington desired. He would also announce his intention to resign from the firm.

Brynn had set Jared on his feet, and the boy was tugging her toward the door as fast as his chubby legs would carry him.

"Gots cars, Bwynn," he was saying. "Lots of 'em."

Rand shook off thoughts of business and followed Brynn and Jared inside.

BRYNN LAY on her stomach in front of the flickering fire, her face just inches from Jared's as they pushed Matchbox cars around several feet of figure-eight track she'd assembled earlier.

She glanced over at Rand, who was watching them from the corner of the sectional. "Join us. This is fun. Right, Jared?"

"Wight." The little boy's face was scrunched in concentration as he maneuvered his car around the course.

"Sorry," Rand said. "I'm better off watching."

"Too old to get down on the floor?" she challenged.

He shook his head. "Just never got the hang of playing."

She halted the progress of her toy and stared at him in disbelief. "Every kid plays."

"This one didn't."

Leaving Jared to his race, she sat cross-legged and studied Rand's face, half-hidden in the shadows with the only light in the room coming from the dancing flames in the fireplace.

"You and your brother never played?" she asked.

"We were…closely supervised."

"By Lillian? I can't believe she didn't encourage you to have fun."

His lips lifted in a sad smile. "Lillian tried to have us play like normal little boys, God bless her. But my parents were very strict. They gave her lists of activities that were acceptable and warned, if she deviated, she'd be fired."

"Brrrden, brrrden." Oblivious to their conversation, Jared made motor noises and rolled his car up the plastic ramp.

Brynn's heart ached for the children Rand and Patrick had been. "What did you do for fun?"

"We rode our ponies, went for sedate walks in the garden, were taken to museums and concerts." Rand's voice was devoid of emotion.

"You were *brothers.* You never wrestled, tumbled on the floor and beat the tar out of each another?" she asked, unable to comprehend the regimen he'd described.

Rand twisted his lips in a wry smile. "We were supposed to be *civilized,* one of Mother's favorite words."

"I didn't realize rich kids could be so deprived," Brynn said in astonishment. "Next you'll tell me you never ate peanut butter and jelly sandwiches."

"We didn't."

She found herself sputtering in surprise. "That's... un-American."

His smile held a latent sadness. "My parents are very cosmopolitan."

More like anal retentive, Brynn thought, but didn't say it aloud. "Were you unhappy?"

"Patrick and I had each other," Rand said, as if avoiding her real question, "and because we were so isolated, until we were sent to boarding school, we didn't know what we were missing. Not even then, really. Most of the other boys came from homes like ours. That's why my parents chose that particular school. It encouraged discipline and decorum."

Brynn shook her head, remembering her past. "I can't picture such a childhood."

"Aiieeee!" Five-year-old Brynn screeched with glee as her father tossed her into the air and caught her in his strong arms, one of their favorite games.

"Do it again, Daddy," Brynn begged.

"Not now," Aunt Marion called. "It's time to eat."

Her father swung her over his head, and with her legs around his shoulders and her hands clasping his hair, galloped toward the picnic table under the shade of a spreading persimmon tree in the backyard. Lucky followed, barking and running in circles.

Nearby, an ice-filled galvanized tub cooled a watermelon and soft drinks, and the table, spread with a red-checkered cloth, held fried chicken, potato salad, a frosty pitcher of iced tea and Aunt Marion's famous red velvet cake.

Brynn's dad shifted her to a seat at the table and heaped her plate with food.

"Can we play s'more after we eat?" Brynn asked.

"After a nap," her father said.

"But, Daddy, I like to swing—"

"Me, too, pumpkin—" he ruffled her curls with his big hand. "But you have to let your meal settle."

"And I have a surprise for you after lunch," Uncle Bud said.

More interested in play than food, Brynn had only picked at her meal, but Uncle Bud had given her a treat anyway, her favorite: a grape Popsicle.

Brynn had found a spot in the sun on the back porch steps and had licked as fast as she could, but she was no match for the mid-July heat. She glanced down to find half the Popsicle had melted, leaving a huge purple stain on her brand-new pink shirt.

"Oh, no!" She glanced to her father, still seated at the table. "I'm sorry, Daddy."

"It's okay, pumpkin."

"But it's my new shirt."

"It's just a stain," he said with a laugh. "It'll come out in the wash. And if it doesn't, we'll buy another shirt. Now enjoy the rest of your Popsicle before it melts, too."

At the memory, Brynn's heart filled with love for her father. Even though he'd had to raise her alone, he'd made certain her childhood was as normal as possible. She'd roughhoused with friends, made mud pies with Jodie and Merrilee, tromped through the woods and pastures with Lucky, had even been the first girl in Pleasant Valley to play on a Little League baseball team. Rand's childhood, privileged as it had been, sounded sterile by comparison.

She hopped to her feet, grabbed his hand, and tugged him from the sofa. "It's never too late."

"Too late for what?"

She handed him a car and pulled him down beside Jared. "To learn to play. Okay, guys, we're going to have a NASCAR race. Gentlemen, start your engines!"

For a second, Rand looked as if she'd asked him to jump off a bridge. Then he took a deep breath, blew it out and placed his car next to Jared's.

"Okay, tiger. Wanna race?"

"Brrrrden, brrrden."

Rand slithered onto his stomach. "Brrrden, brrden."

His arms were longer, his reflexes faster, but he let Jared win.

Half an hour later, with Jared asleep in his arms, Rand climbed the stairs to tuck him in while Brynn picked up the track and cars and stowed them in a plastic bin.

In a few minutes, Rand returned. "He's out like a light."

"He's a good kid."

"The best. I just hope I can give him what he needs."

"Just love him, spend time with him, and he'll be fine."

"Voice of experience?" Rand sank into the sofa and pulled her down beside him.

Brynn shrugged. "That's what my dad did for me. As far as I know, I don't have any emotional scars. Although I do wish I'd known my mother. I have only vague memories."

"Jared's so young, he may not remember his parents at all."

"You must have pictures, videos?"

"Only ones that Patrick took." His expression darkened and pain filled his eyes. "My biggest regret is that I didn't spend more time with my brother and his family."

She wanted to smooth the worried creases from his forehead, but didn't trust herself to touch him, afraid where it might lead. "I've heard Gofer tell the Archer Farm boys that you can drive yourself crazy with shoulda, woulda, coulda. He says you have to live for the present and the future."

"Gofer sounds like a smart man." His tone was wistful, almost envious.

"You were great with Jared tonight." Enmeshed in the realization that he still held her hand, she struggled to concentrate on conversation.

"You really think so?" Rand, who'd always seemed so confident and self-assured, sounded vulnerable.

Suddenly tongue-tied with emotions she couldn't— didn't want—to name, Brynn nodded.

Rand cupped her face with his hands. "You are amazing."

White-hot need flared deep in her stomach, like a match touched to dry kindling. She'd been drawn to Rand since the first time she had seen him in the snow on Valley Road. Not only was he extremely easy on the eyes, he'd captivated her with his devotion to his nephew, his many kindnesses toward his neighbors. A powerful and successful man, he'd put his high-powered career on hold to take care of Jared, and he'd done it without complaint. And with a hint of vulnerability that exposed his deep humanity. Unlike other men she'd dated, had even slid between the sheets with, Rand was special.

In spite of herself, she loved him.

But the fire that built in her now was more than love. She blazed with need, a pure lust that longed to translate her feelings into physical form. When his hands moved to her hair, and his fingers combed out her braid and fluffed her curls around her face, her breath caught in her throat. She couldn't tell him to stop. Didn't want him to stop.

"I've never met anyone like you." Rand's breath fanned her cheek, and his gaze locked with hers, the brown in his eyes like swirls of melted chocolate, throwing off heat.

"That could be good or bad," she replied, struggling to breathe past the emotion that clogged her throat.

"Oh, it's good. It's very, very good."

And joining her body with his would be more than good.

It would be commitment, she realized with a jolt

as electric as the heat of his hands. And what would she do when he returned to New York? She couldn't leave the valley. Didn't belong in the cosmopolitan world he'd come from.

He'd slid his hands beneath her sweater and with a single motion, swept it over her head. She wore nothing beneath but a wisp of lacy bra.

Stop now, before it's too late, her head warned.

But her heart wasn't listening, and she wanted him with every cell of her being crying out for his touch. She slipped her hands beneath the rich fabric of his shirt, felt the rapid thud of his heart beneath her palms.

All reason snapped, and lust, wild and wanton, took its place.

His lips claimed hers, and in a frenzied dance, they stripped each other's clothes while their mouths joined, mingling breath, desire and desperate need. Her hands roamed his nakedness, skimmed the tautness of his muscles, the curve of his buttocks, the hardness of his arousal.

With a guttural moan, Rand scooped her in his arms, carried her to the fireplace, and laid her on the thick sheepskin rug. He arched above her, his body golden in the firelight, passion burning in his eyes.

"Brynn." He breathed her name like a prayer. "Are you sure?"

She didn't hesitate. "I've never been more certain."

He shook his head, as if waking from a dream, and bent to kiss her. "Don't move. I'll be right back."

He was gone, but the fire warmed her, and in an

instant he returned, clasping a foil-wrapped condom. She noted with satisfaction that his hands trembled as he put it on, a reflection of her corresponding shiver of anticipation.

Driven by the hunger that consumed them, they abandoned foreplay and he entered her. Her legs encircled him and their bodies rocked in a primeval rhythm that flooded her with mind-blowing pleasure. The fire beside them mirrored the one inside them—surging, engulfing and carrying them on a wave of heat until they exploded in a conflagration that consumed body and mind.

Later, propped above her on his elbows, Rand gazed into her eyes. "You're even more amazing than I'd imagined."

I love you, she thought, but couldn't voice the words. Love, in her book, was forever. And Rand, no matter how much she cared for him, was only passing through.

He shifted beside her and drew her into his arms with the lean, hard length of his body cuddled against hers. Sated and exhausted from the fervor of their lovemaking, she snuggled against him, savoring the moment.

Oh, lordy, she thought. *What have I gone and done?*

Chapter Ten

The next morning, Rand awoke and reached for Brynn again. But he was in his own bed, and the other side was empty, even though a hint of floral fragrance clung to the pillow beside him.

Last night had been incredible. He'd had sexual partners before, but never until now, he realized, had he made love to a woman. His first time with Brynn had happened so fast, it was over almost as soon as it had begun. But the second time, here in the soft comfort of his king-size bed with only moonlight and the sound of the river streaming through the open French doors, he'd loved her with the slow, caressing thoroughness that she deserved.

Holding her in his arms afterward had seemed like the culmination of a desire he'd nurtured his entire life, and he hadn't wanted to let her go.

"Spend the night," he'd begged.

She shook her head, tickling his nose with her hair. "I have to work an early shift."

"Call in sick."

She'd lifted herself on one elbow and skewered him with an outraged look. *One* eye, at least, had held outrage. The other had been hidden behind a curtain of magnificent auburn tresses, wild and tangled by his hands.

"I'm not sick. I can't lie."

"I know. I was just thinking wishfully." He'd smiled and drawn her to him again. One of the things he loved about Brynn was her innate sense of right and wrong. She was incapable of being dishonest.

Was that why she hadn't said she loved him? He'd wanted to proclaim his own feelings, but fear had held him back, fear he'd spook her if he revealed the depth of his emotions too soon.

He drew the abandoned pillow with her scent against him and inhaled deeply, as reluctant to let the smell of her go as he had been to release her. Patience, he counseled himself. Slow and steady wins the prize. And Brynn was as fine a prize as any man could ever hope for.

The no-nonsense tread of Lillian's shoes sounded in the upstairs hall. Rand glanced at the clock and realized he'd overslept. He flung off the covers, swung his feet to the floor and headed for the shower.

An hour later, dressed in clean clothes and with Lillian's hearty breakfast under his belt, he climbed the stairs to his study to return Charles Steinman's call.

"Rand, good to hear from you." Steinman's too-hearty tone reverberated through the phone after Rand had run the gauntlet of switchboard, secretary and personal assistant to reach the senior partner. "Farrington's chomping at the bit. Wants to know how soon you can cinch the deals on that acreage."

"I can't."

A moment of dead silence hung in the air. "Sorry, Rand. I don't think I heard you correctly."

"You heard me, Charles. Buying the acreage in Pleasant Valley isn't going to happen."

"Why not? If you need more money for leverage—"

"Money won't help," Rand said. "These people are connected to their land through generations that go back before the Revolutionary War. They won't sell at any price."

"None of them?"

"Certainly not Joe Mauney or Eileen Bickerstaff."

Steinman's curse rang in his ear. "There're not enough contiguous smaller farms to make up the area we need. The Bickerstaff and Mauney farms were our only hope."

"Sorry, Charles."

"Sorry? That's all you can say? Where's that ruthless competitive spirit you're so famous for?" He spoke again before Rand could answer. "Are you feeling all right?"

"Actually, I feel better than I've felt in my whole life."

"Maybe if I send Laudermann—"

"You could send the 82nd Airborne and it won't make any difference. These people won't sell." Rand took a deep breath before launching into his next point. "I'm overnighting my resignation—"

"What?" Steinman sounded genuinely distressed. "You're not serious."

"I'm completely serious."

"But, dammit, Rand, you're one of the best in the firm. You can't take this setback personally."

"I don't. I—"

"Don't do anything hasty. Let me talk to Farrington. See what he wants to do. There may be other equally suitable spots nearby you can go after."

Rand hesitated. He'd had enough of subterfuge. But he'd promised Steinman and Farrington he'd do his best. As long as he could stay in Pleasant Valley with Jared and Brynn, he didn't have to resign. Yet.

"I'll hold off on resigning. If Farrington wants me to investigate other properties, let me know."

"I'll be in touch." Steinman cut the connection.

Rand returned the handset to its cradle and stared across the valley. In the distance, the rolling hills of Eileen Bickerstaff's farm lifted toward the mountains, the orchards on their slopes thick with blossoms, giving the illusion of drifting snow. The peacefulness of the sight loosened the tension in his gut formed by his conversation with Steinman.

With a start, Rand realized it had been weeks since he'd resorted to popping antacids by the hour. Maybe, he thought with a smile, if he stayed in Pleasant Valley, he could throw away the whole damned bottle.

A WAVE OF EXCITEMENT flitted through Brynn's stomach like a cluster of drug-crazed butterflies. She hadn't seen Rand since leaving him asleep early Tuesday morning, and the closer to River Walk she drove, the greater her anticipation grew.

She'd talked with him on the phone the past few days, but work had kept her too busy for more than the briefest of conversations. But memories of their lovemaking had consumed her thoughts throughout the week. She'd spent Tuesday investigating a B&E— breaking and entering—a couple blocks down Mountain Street from her home, where a computer and DVD player had been stolen. Wednesday she and Lucas Rhodes had answered a call about a domestic dispute at the trailer park on the edge of town on the Carsons Corner highway. They'd disarmed the drunken husband of his knife, arrested him and driven his battered wife to the E.R. for stitches in her forearm.

Thursday, Rand had called with an invitation to a birthday party for Jared on Saturday, and, in between paperwork and rousting a stray cow from Mrs. Fulton's flower beds, Brynn had racked her brains for a suitable gift for the little boy.

She had mixed feelings about the party. On the

one hand, the presence of Jodie and Jeff and Grant and Merrilee would prevent a repeat of Monday night's incredible lovemaking, a good thing, since Brynn shouldn't have allowed things to progress that far in the first place. On the other hand, since she'd left Rand's bed Tuesday morning, all she could think of was seeing him again, watching him smile, hearing his voice….

"Hey, Brynn, you still with us?" She looked up to see Lucas standing in the office doorway. Lucas had grown up in the valley, too, although a few years ahead of Brynn. Muscular, dedicated and with rugged good looks, the man someday was going to break some woman's heart—if he hadn't already. Lord knew, Aunt Marion had tried hard enough to throw Brynn and Lucas together, but they were just friends. Good friends.

"What did you say?" Brynn asked.

"I asked about the paperwork on that domestic abuse, but you were miles away."

She fumbled for an excuse for her daydreaming. "You were a little boy."

He folded his arms over his chest and leaned against the door frame. An easy grin crossed his face. "Last time I looked."

"I need a birthday present for a two-year-old boy, and I haven't got a clue."

"Does he like cars?"

Brynn rolled her eyes. "He's too young to drive."

"I'm serious."

"Yeah, he loves cars."

"Then stop by my place when you get off work. I may have just what you're looking for."

With any other man, Brynn would have considered the offer a come-on, but she and Lucas had been partners and buddies too long to believe his suggestion anything other than a genuine desire to be helpful.

And he'd been right on the money. Together they'd stashed his handiwork into the back of Brynn's SUV, where it rode now, covered with a tarp. The moment she'd laid eyes on it, she'd known it was the perfect gift, but the closer she drew to River Walk, the more her reservations grew. What if Jared didn't like it?

Even more nerve-wracking were her thoughts of Rand. With her best friends and their husbands present, how was Brynn supposed to remain nonchalant? She didn't want to hurt Rand's feelings by seeming aloof, but she didn't want Merrilee and Jodie to guess what was happening between Rand and her, either. Especially since Brynn wasn't sure exactly what *was* happening or where it would lead.

She parked on the landing behind Jodie's van and hurried around the house to the main deck overlooking the river. Jodie and Jeff stood talking with Rand, and her heart stuttered at the heat in Rand's eyes when he spotted her.

He looked more handsome than ever in jeans slung low on his narrow hips and a rugby shirt with broad red-and-blue stripes. A breeze off the river ruffled his fine hair, and a web of tiny lines formed at the corners of his eyes where he squinted in the bright sunlight. He had been leaning with his back against the rail, his hands braced on the banister, straining the muscles of his biceps against the fabric of his sleeves. His gaze held hers until Jared streaked past him, and Rand pushed away from the railing to follow the boy.

"Bwynn!" Jared raced toward her and she braced herself for his hug. "It's my bifday!"

She knelt beside him and returned his embrace. "I know, sweetie. Happy Birthday. I have a surprise for you."

He drew back and looked her over from head to toe. "Where? In your pocket? Is it little?"

"Oh, no," Brynn said with a laugh. "It's big. We'll need Uncle Rand and Jeff to carry it."

"You want a hand?" Rand asked.

Along with all the rest of you, Brynn thought longingly, and nodded.

Jeff and Jodie joined them.

"I can help, too," Jeff said.

"Maybe we should wait till after lunch," Brynn suggested with a questioning look at Rand.

"Now's as good a time as any," Rand said with a nod at Jared, who was hopping from one foot to the other with excitement. "Don't know if he can take the suspense much longer."

Brynn keyed the SUV's remote and unlocked the hatch. "It's in the back."

She climbed to the main deck and, holding Jared

in her arms to keep him from underfoot, stood with Jodie while the men removed the tarp-wrapped item slightly larger than a steamer trunk from her car and manhandled it up to the deck.

"What's under that thing?" Jodie asked.

"Lucas made it in his woodworking shop," Brynn explained. "He'd intended to sell it at the Daffodil Days flea market but it wasn't finished in time. Lucky for me. I just hope Jared likes it."

Rand and Jeff set the bundle on the floor of the deck, and Brynn placed Jared on his feet.

"Ready, tiger?" Rand asked.

He and Jeff had loosened the tarp in preparation for the unveiling.

"Weady," Jared said. He clasped his hands and held his breath.

"Tah-dah!" Rand exclaimed, as the men whipped the tarp aside, then added, "Wow," when he had a look at what he'd uncovered.

"A car!" Jared squealed with delight and ran toward the sleek wooden replica of a NASCAR racer, complete with shining red paint, an identifying numeral and even a steering wheel that moved.

The large tires rotated also, but only if someone pushed from behind.

"It's a combination car and toy chest," Brynn explained. "After you're through playing in it, you can store your toys."

Jared clambered into the driver's seat, gripped

the steering wheel, and spun it first left, then right. "Brrrden, brrrden."

Rand's gaze met hers over the boy's head. "It's perfect."

"This'll be a hard act to follow." Jeff squatted on his knees to admire the car's workmanship and ran a hand over the car's sleek lines.

"Under other circumstances, I'd be worried," Rand said, "but here comes my gift now."

Grant's pickup had pulled into a parking place on the landing, and Merrilee and Grant climbed out. Grant reached behind the driver's seat for a large cardboard box that he tucked beneath his arm.

The new arrivals exchanged greetings and admired Brynn's gift. Grant handed the box to Rand.

"Jared." Rand set the box on the deck. "I have a present for you."

Jared eyed the box with curiosity, but clung to the steering wheel of his racer, reluctant to let go. When the box on the deck jiggled slightly and a muffled sound emanated from it, the boy's curiosity won out. He climbed out of the car and approached the box, interested but skeptical. "Is it a beah?"

"No, not a bear," Rand said.

"What is it?"

"Look and see, tiger. It won't hurt you. I promise."

Rand knelt with his arm around the boy as Jared folded back the flaps of the box.

"A puppy!" Jared reached into the cardboard container and withdrew a wiggling brown bundle of fur that immediately licked his face.

"She's a chocolate Lab," Grant explained.

"She'll need a name," Brynn said. Watching Rand watching Jared made her insides warm and tingly.

"Candy," Jared said, "'cause she's choc'late?"

"What kind of candy?" Rand asked.

"Snickers," Jared replied instantly.

"I think," Grant said with approval, "that Snickers is a perfect name. And Snickers is housebroken and has had all her shots."

"Another rescue?" Brynn asked.

The vet nodded. "Rand contacted me early last week and Snickers arrived yesterday, just in time. Although I have to admit, Gloria, spoiled rotten dog that she is, didn't want to see her leave. She thought we'd brought her a playmate."

"Gloria will have a playmate soon enough," Merrilee announced with a glowing look.

Grant put his arm around Merrilee's shoulder and drew her to him, and they fielded a flood of congratulations.

A lump formed in Brynn's throat. Grant had fallen in love with Merrilee over seven years ago, but Merrilee had taken off for New York and a career. Only a family crisis had brought her home and them back together, and now they were expecting a family of their own.

A family...

She turned her attention to Rand and Jared, both sitting on the deck and playing with Snickers. Longing burrowed through her. She wanted Rand in her life, and Jared, too. Within the longing, another emotion flickered. Hope. Maybe, just maybe, things would work out for Brynn and Rand. After all, prospects for Grant and Merrilee had seemed grim for a long, long time, but look at them now, happily married and expecting their first child.

She closed her eyes with the sun on her face, the breeze in her hair, the twitter of birds in her ears and the fragrance of flowers filling her nostrils. The promise of spring: new life, new beginnings.

Brynn opened her eyes to find Rand's gaze on hers. His eyes were filled with promise, too.

IT WAS ALMOST midnight when Brynn drove away from River Walk. Rand's goodbye kiss and the remembrance of his arms around her still warmed her.

She'd been the last to leave. Rand had asked her to stay the night, but she'd declined, explaining that their relationship was moving too fast, that she wanted to take things slower to make sure they didn't ruin a good thing by rushing it. She'd loved him all the more when he'd understood.

Jared's party had been a huge success. Rand had fit in easily with Jeff and Jodie and Grant and Merrilee, and they had shared stories, jokes and laughter as they lazed on the deck and watched Jared, playing with his new puppy and his race car.

Rand had even exhibited his newfound skill as a chef, preparing steaks and vegetables on the impressive outdoor grill. Lillian had provided a bottomless pitcher of sangria and a huge birthday cake for Jared, and, sated with good food and drink and surrounded by her favorite people, Brynn had experienced a perfect day.

Wrapped in a glow of contentment, she pulled into the driveway of her house. She was so preoccupied with memories of the day that she took a moment to realize something was wrong. Lights streamed from every window, and Uncle Bud's car was parked behind her father's in front of the garage.

Her heart hammered in her chest. Neither her dad nor Uncle Bud was a night owl. Staying up so late meant only one thing: a crisis. A dozen dire alternatives surged through her thoughts, but her main concern was for her father.

Brynn parked the SUV and hurried inside. To her immense relief, her father and Uncle Bud were sitting in the living room and stood when she entered. A quick scrutiny assured her that her father appeared healthy, although his usually genial expression was grim.

"What's wrong?" she asked and glanced around the room. "Where's Aunt Marion?"

"Marion's at home. She's fine," Uncle Bud answered quickly, "but we need to talk to you."

"Me?" Brynn glanced from her uncle to her father. Both men met her gaze with somber expressions. "About what?"

Her father ran his hand through his thick silver hair and grabbed the back of his neck. His blue eyes, so like her own, burrowed through her. "Tell us, pumpkin, just how much do you know about this Randall Benedict?"

Chapter Eleven

Hunt and Bud Sawyer were an unlikely pair of brothers. Bud, the older, was short with a wrestler's build, a perpetual smile and a fringe of gray hair surrounding his bald pate, giving him the appearance of the Friar Tuck character from old Robin Hood movies. Hunt, tall and lean with a quiet dignity, looked more like an elder statesman than a small town police chief.

Tonight both shared the same worried expression. If Brynn hadn't known better, she'd have thought her father and uncle had waited up, determined to defend the virtue of the youngest female of their clan, but both men knew Brynn could take care of herself. Something other than Brynn's reputation was troubling them.

Something to do with Rand. And from the scowls on their faces, that something wasn't good.

"You both know as much as I do about Rand Benedict," she hedged, shoving aside intimate memories. "He's the attorney from New York who bought

River Walk. He's staying there with his nephew, his ward, while on sabbatical from his law practice."

Uncle Bud's frown deepened and drew his bushy eyebrows together. "You sure he's on sabbatical?"

"Except for drawing up Eileen Bickerstaff's will," Brynn admitted, "but that was a personal favor, not a work assignment. What's got you two riled up?"

"Sit down, pumpkin." Her dad waved her toward a chair and folded his own tall frame into his usual seat by the fireplace.

Brynn took the chair across from her father, but Uncle Bud continued standing and paced the rug.

"I just got back," Bud said, "from a meeting of the Upstate Chambers of Commerce. Learned that the folks around Westminster had a problem a while back. Some lawyer representing Farrington Properties tried to buy a couple thousand acres of lakeside acreage."

Determined not to draw conclusions before she had all the facts, Brynn leaned back in her chair and forced the tension from her muscles with a deeply drawn breath. "Trying to buy land's not illegal, is it?"

"No, but this fellow's approach was under-handed," her father said. "According to Bud's source, the man wasn't open about what he was doing. Claimed to be looking for property for a home for himself. One of the locals got suspicious at the amount of land he wanted to accumulate, did some snooping and discovered the guy worked for Far-rington, who builds huge retirement villages with adjacent megamalls. Turned out the attorney didn't want the property for himself, but for Farrington to develop."

Bud nodded with a grimace. "They say one lawyer with a briefcase can steal more than a hundred men with guns."

Brynn looked at her uncle in surprise. "I never thought I'd hear you quoting Don Corleone."

"You taught me that *Godfather* quote," Bud said. "It's the only one of your many cracks about lawyers that I remember."

A sinking sensation drifted down into Brynn's stomach. "What's this Westminster problem have to do with Rand?"

"When the folks there got wind of Farrington's intentions," Bud said, "it quashed the deals. Farrington decided to look elsewhere to build his retirement village in the Upstate."

"You don't mean here, in Pleasant Valley?" She winced at the prospect of development blighting the valley's beauty.

"Just think what thousands of acres of retirement homes would do to the rural life we enjoy so much," her father said.

Brynn turned to her uncle. "But you're always saying more people are better for business."

Bud shook his head. "Not that many people. They'd clog the roads with traffic, create air pollution with their cars. And a megamall with national chains could offer lower prices and put the local merchants out of business."

"What makes you think Rand's a part of this?" He couldn't be, Brynn thought, not the Rand who seemed to appreciate the valley so much. Not the Rand she'd come to love.

Bud threw her a sympathetic look. "I went online after the conference. Did a Google search for Farrington Properties. I found out the company fired the law firm that botched the Westminster acquisitions."

"Rand's firm?" Uneasiness sat heavy in her stomach like an undigested meal. The inconsistencies about Rand's presence in the valley that she'd shoved to the back of her mind returned in a rush.

Buying a house far too big for two, a trout-fishing paradise even though he didn't like to fish. A workaholic on sabbatical. His many questions about the Bickerstaff and Mauney farms.

Uncle Bud shook his head. "After failing in Westminster, Farrington fired his old law firm and engaged new representation with Steinman, Slagle and Crump in Manhattan. And guess who's listed in their registry?"

"Randall Benedict, Esquire," her father said.

"It must be coincidence," Brynn insisted. The alternative sickened her.

"I don't think so," her dad said grimly. "Your years in law enforcement have taught you not to think so, either. Coincidences are rarer than hen's teeth."

"You want me to talk to him?" Brynn looked from her father to Bud and back again. "I'll just ask him flat out if he's here to buy property for Farrington."

"Would he tell you the truth if he is?" her father said with a gentleness that suggested he'd guessed her feelings for Rand.

Confusion smothered her like a blanket. If Rand wasn't Farrington's point man, he'd say so. But if he was? Would he tell her the truth after keeping it from her all this time? And if he was in the valley just to buy property, had his interest in her been merely part of his cover, along with buying River Walk and using Jared's health as an excuse for coming to this particular place? Had she been just a diversion to pass the time while he waited to close his deal?

She slumped in her chair. "What do you want me to do?"

"Take a vacation," her father said unexpectedly.

"What?"

"I'll bring Sid Peeler out of retirement to cover your shifts. I want you to spend every available minute with this Benedict, see if you can dig out what he's up to."

"If he's here to buy property for Farrington," Bud said, "we need to find out if he's had any success. And we should get out the word, alert people to the consequences to the entire community if we let that developer get a foothold in the valley."

The hope Brynn had felt earlier in the day shattered, and its loss left a bitter taste in her mouth. How could she spend time with Rand as if nothing had changed, when *everything* had?

"Think about it." Uncle Bud headed for the door. "You've spent more time with Benedict than the rest of us. Maybe he'll trust you with his secrets. I'd better head home. Marion wants to attend the early worship service tomorrow."

Lost in dark and dreary thoughts, Brynn was barely aware of her uncle's departure or her father's presence. She jumped, startled, when her dad sat on the arm of her chair and put his arm around her.

"Want to tell me about it?" he asked.

"About what?"

"From the look on your face, I think you've grown to care quite a bit about this Benedict fellow."

She leaned against her father's broad shoulders. Her entire life he had been her bulwark, a steady comforting influence whenever she was troubled or unhappy. He'd always listened to her problems without judgment or criticism. His faithful quiet presence had spoken volumes of his love and acceptance. She had lost her mother too soon, but her father, with his calm strength and tender understanding, had done all a man could do to fill that void.

"I thought I was in love with him, Daddy." Uncertainty gripped her. "But if you and Uncle Bud are right, how can I care for someone I don't really know?"

"Don't you think you'd better find out the truth?

Not only for the sake of our friends in the valley, but for your own peace of mind?"

She shook her head. "I don't want to be around him. Everything's changed now. And I'm not very good at pretending it hasn't."

Her father squeezed her shoulders. "Then don't pretend. Just be yourself. And remember that everything happens for a reason."

Brynn pushed to her feet, kissed her father goodnight and climbed the stairs to her room. She'd met Rand for a purpose. Of that she was absolutely sure. But whether that purpose was to fall in love or merely to expose his schemes, she had yet to determine.

BIRDS SANG in the dogwood trees outside her bedroom window early the next morning, and, although she'd had only a few hours sleep, Brynn was instantly alert—prodded to immediate wakefulness by memories of last night's disturbing discussion with her father and uncle.

Through the window that overlooked the backyard, she could see her father puttering in the garden, the knees of his jeans damp with early morning dew. He selected a plant from a flat of pansies at his side, dug a hole with his trowel and tucked the seedling along the border in front of the candy-stripe tulips whose flowers were beginning to fade.

According to Aunt Marion, Brynn's best source of information on her mother, flowers had always been her mother's passion. Her father rarely spoke of his late wife, seeming to find it difficult. But actions sometimes spoke louder than words. After her mother's death, Hunt had taken over the care of the rose garden, the azaleas and perennial beds a silent but ongoing tribute to the memory of his wife. After a respectful period of mourning had passed, Aunt Marion had tried to hook her brother-in-law up with other women, but Hunt Sawyer had shook his head and declined all offers.

"No one could replace your mother. And besides, I like my solitude." He spent his spare time tending his wife's flowers with the same love and devotion he'd once given her and seemed happiest alone in the garden with his memories.

The ring of the telephone on her bedside table drew Brynn's attention from her father in the garden. Hoping it wasn't a call that would require either of them to work on Sunday, Brynn answered.

"Good morning." The rich, deep tones of Rand's voice caressed her ear and sent a buzz of awareness along her nerves like a low-voltage shock. She remembered the heat that curled in her stomach at his smile, the tantalizing depths of his brown eyes, the intoxicating taste of his kiss, the sensuous magic of his hands…and the nasty suspicions her father and uncle had raised.

"Hello." Distrust poured through her, destroying the comfort she'd felt with Rand before Uncle Bud's revelations. "You're up early."

"It's a beautiful day. Want to drive into the mountains and have lunch with me?"

She had to bite back an instant no. For her own sake, if no one else's, she had to find where she stood with Rand. She'd given him her heart, her body, her trust. One of the talents that made her a good cop was her instincts. She had to prove to herself whether those instincts had failed her in judging Rand's character. If he was here to cause trouble, she had to expose him. And if he wasn't in the valley under false pretenses, her sense of fair play insisted that she clear his name.

"Hello? You still there?"

"I'd love a drive in the mountains," she answered quickly and hoped her voice held the appropriate enthusiasm.

"I'll pick you up—"

"No need to drive into town and double back. I can meet you at River Walk."

"You're sure? I don't mind—"

"It will give me a chance to see Jared." *And maybe to snoop around.*

"The inn I have in mind is a couple hours away. Will ten thirty be too early?"

Brynn glanced at the clock. She'd have just enough time to shower and dress. "I'll see you then."

EXACTLY ON TIME, Brynn rang the bell at River Walk. Lillian answered the door with Jared and a boisterous Snickers at her heels. Brynn knelt to greet the boy and his dog. One hugged her. The other bathed her face with sloppy kisses. She returned the boy's hug with a fierce embrace, knowing she'd grown too fond of him, and that losing him would hurt as much as losing Rand.

"Mr. Benedict will be with you in a few moments," Lillian said. "He's checking an electrical problem in the guest house."

Brynn released Jared, gazed up at the housekeeper and raised her eyebrows. "I thought he wasn't much of a handyman."

"Even an attorney should be able to sort out a tripped circuit," Lillian answered with a twinkle in her green eyes.

"Bwynn." Jared tugged her to her feet. "Come see my car."

Brynn looked to Lillian. "Do I have time?"

Lillian nodded. "Mr. Benedict moved it upstairs to Jared's room. He's been a very good boy about putting away his toys in such an unusual toy box."

With Jared's chubby hand in hers and Snickers dogging their steps, Brynn climbed to the second floor and tried not to think of the last time she'd ascended those stairs, cradled in Rand's arms.

The boy led her to the doorway of his room. Tucked beneath the windows that overlooked the river stood the racer Lucas had built, its bright red paint shining in the morning sun. Spotting the car, Jared dropped her hand, rushed to the toy chest and began tossing toys out of the driver's seat onto the floor as if he'd forgotten she was there.

Brynn pivoted and glanced into the open doorway behind her. Rand's study. The surface of his huge desk was uncluttered except for a telephone, a bronze statue of an eagle and a large roll of paper. Her stomach knotted in anxiety, but her course was clear.

Moving quickly, Brynn entered the study, grabbed the paper and unrolled it onto the desk's broad surface. She recognized instantly the contours and roads of Pleasant Valley. And the Mauney and Bickerstaff properties were outlined on the map in red.

Uncle Bud had been right, she thought with a sinking heart and a sick feeling in her stomach. Rand had come to the valley to buy property and, while that goal in itself wasn't a crime, the sneaky, underhanded way he'd gone about it was exactly what Brynn would expect from a lawyer—a *Yankee* lawyer. So much for Rand's changing her attitude toward his profession. Instead, his deception had validated all her prejudices.

And broken her heart.

At the sound of a door closing downstairs, she rolled up the map and hurried from the study into Jared's room. Rand found her there seconds later, kneeling on the floor beside Jared in his racer. Her heart was thudding in her ears, and her face burned with shame, both at her snooping and her gullibility.

"Sorry to keep you waiting," he said, his voice cheerful, his expression warm and welcoming. Too welcoming. She exerted all her self-control to keep from throwing herself into his arms and begging him to tell her she'd misunderstood the evidence on his desk.

Instead, she forced her lips to smile. "No problem. Jared and I have been having fun. Right, Jared?"

Jared, tiny hands gripping the steering wheel, his thoughts obviously on some imaginary racetrack, nodded distractedly.

"We'd better get started then." Rand held out his hand.

Brynn grasped it and allowed him to pull her to her feet. She silently cursed the tingle of awareness that coursed through her veins. Apparently her traitorous body hadn't caught up with her mind's assessment of Rand.

Unaware of her turmoil, he squeezed her hand. "It's a perfect day for a drive."

He tucked her arm through his, walked with her down the stairs and out the wide front entrance, and opened the door of the Jaguar for her to climb in before sliding behind the wheel.

"Where exactly are we going?" Brynn asked, surprised by the steadiness of her voice when her thoughts and emotions were roiling in chaos. "Asheville?"

Rand started the engine and headed the car toward the highway. "Not that far. The Balsam Mountain Inn is this side of Waynesville. Lillian read about it in *Southern Living* while she was having her hair done in town. Ever been to the inn?"

Brynn shook her head and wished Rand didn't look so irresistible in expensive black slacks and a dove-gray sweater that molded the enticing contours of his chest. If he had any qualms about his schemes for the valley, they didn't show in his demeanor. He acted like a man at peace with the world.

"I really like Grant and Merrilee," he commented as they passed the entrance to the Nathans' driveway. "And Snickers couldn't be more perfect for Jared. Grant knows his animals."

"The puppy has certainly lifted Jared's spirits. He laughs a lot more now." Thinking of Jared doubled Brynn's sense of loss and made her realize how she'd already begun to think of Rand and Jared as her family, a future that definitely wasn't going to happen after her discovery in Rand's study.

They rode in silence, the familiar landscape of the valley streaming past her window, until they reached Blackberry Farm.

"Next time we head for the hills," Rand said, "we'll invite Eileen. She's a remarkable woman, but she doesn't get out often enough."

Painfully aware there wouldn't be a next time, Brynn faked another smile. "Eileen would like that. Although she lives alone, she enjoys other people's company."

"I hadn't realized her property is so extensive,"

Rand said casually. The man apparently had no conscience, because Brynn could detect no guilt in his tone. "She told me there are two other houses on it, in addition to the main house."

Brynn stifled a groan. Drawing up Eileen's will had given Rand the perfect opportunity to pry. "Eileen used to hire workers who lived on the farm, but that was years ago. The houses are probably in shambles now."

Not that Rand would care. She struggled to keep her disgust from showing. Farrington Properties would scrape the acreage bare, bulldozing every structure and tree to build the retirement village.

"Eileen said she'd had the houses inspected recently," Rand added. "They need a few repairs and upgrades, but they're built well and should last a long, long time."

"She had them inspected?" That was news to Brynn. "Is she planning to rent them again?"

Rand shrugged. "She didn't say."

Or maybe the so-called inspection had been a fair market appraisal, Brynn thought, in preparation for a sale. She'd been blunt with Rand before, so she'd try that tack again. "Eileen isn't selling them, is she?"

"No, but I can't say more without violating attorney-client privilege." He cast her an apologetic smile. "Sorry."

Brynn's thoughts whirled in useless circles. All

the evidence against Rand so far was circumstantial, even his own comments. Was his obvious affection for Eileen the result of true appreciation of the remarkable old woman or simply gratitude that she'd agreed to sell him her farm? Brynn intended to find out. So far, she just hadn't figured out how.

RAND CAST A GLANCE at Brynn before returning his gaze to the road. As much as he wanted to feast his eyes on the lovely woman beside him, the narrow, twisting mountain curves demanded his attention. He had passed the turnoff to Archer Farm over ten minutes ago, and he shifted into a lower gear to ease the Jaguar's ascension of the steep grade. At the top, he pulled into a scenic overlook and stopped the car.

"I've never viewed the valley from this angle," he said.

Brynn flashed him a brittle smile, a look that threatened to break into a million tiny pieces, and stepped from the car. She stood at the waist-high stone wall of the overlook with the updraft from the sheer cliff below lifting her glorious hair off the slender column of her neck and molding the delicate fabric of her dress to her body.

Rand recalled vividly every curve, every line of her, and heat pooled in his groin at the memory. The night of their lovemaking she'd been open, relaxed. Happy. But this morning something was wrong. Although her words were warm and her lips curved often into a delectable smile, the warmth never reached her eyes. She was closed off, tense and withdrawn beneath her pleasant facade.

Had he pushed her too far, too fast? He hadn't known how devoid of meaning his life had been until he'd met Brynn. His days had been a dry routine, one much like the other, all infinitely boring, without real purpose. With Brynn, he'd learned to live again, to be the kind of man who could provide the security and affection that Jared needed, a man who could open himself to a woman and include her in his life without reservation. He'd finally recognized his climb to power at the law firm for what it had been: a meaningless, futile attempt to plug the hole in his soul. But Rand didn't need power or prestige. He wanted family, friends and a real home filled with love, acceptance, warmth and laughter.

But Brynn wasn't laughing as she gazed out over Pleasant Valley, stretched five thousand feet below them like a topographic map. Standing on top of the world, she looked as if its weight bore down on her.

He moved behind her, slid his arms around her waist and drew her against him. Unable to resist, he placed his lips against the soft flesh at the back of her neck. She stiffened slightly, then relaxed in his embrace.

"What are you thinking?" he asked, hoping she'd share what was bothering her.

"How much I love the valley." Her voice trembled with emotion.

"I've come to love it, too."

"Have you?" The updraft caught her words and flung them away but not before he noted they were edged with skepticism.

He nodded and buried his face in her hair. "What is it Grant calls this place?"

He felt her quick intake of breath beneath his hands. "Almost Heaven."

Rand gazed down on the patchwork of plowed red fields, snowy orchards and green meadows, bisected by the meandering silver ribbon of the Piedmont River and the corresponding path of the highway. Scattered across the farmland, houses and barns looking no bigger than Monopoly game pieces glistened in the morning sun. At the far end of the valley, church spires in town lifted above the trees and glinted brilliant white against the clear blue sky. Emotions too strong for words shook him. He felt as if he'd died and gone to Heaven, all right. His formerly barren life was behind him, and the future stretched ahead, ripe with promise, just like the valley below in the first flush of spring.

He'd invited Brynn to lunch today to tell her of his plans. He'd faxed his resignation Friday to Steinman, and afterwards he'd called Jodie, met her in town and rented the space above her café as his office. From now on, River Walk in Pleasant Valley would be his home. And he wanted to share that home with Brynn, if she'd have him. Before today, he'd had every confidence that she would. Now, considering her strange demeanor, he wasn't so sure.

The ring of his cell phone jarred him from his thoughts. Not wanting to break the spell of the valley vista, he started not to answer. Concern for Jared, however, had him checking the caller ID. It was Brynn's home number.

"Rand Benedict," he said.

"Put my daughter on," a male voice heavy with authority demanded, omitting the niceties.

Rand handed Brynn the phone. "It's for you."

"Hello," Brynn said. The color left her cheeks as she listened to her father. Suddenly she sagged against the stone wall as if her knees had given way.

Rand grasped her elbow to support her, but she shook him off.

"I'm on my way, Daddy." She switched off the phone and returned it to Rand.

"I have to go," she said.

"Home?"

"No." She strode toward the car and flung open the passenger door. "Blackberry Farm. Someone's attacked Mrs. Bickerstaff."

Chapter Twelve

Rand hurried to the car, turned it back toward the valley and drove as fast as the winding road allowed. Worry for Mrs. Bickerstaff tightened like a vise around Brynn's chest.

"Is Eileen all right?" he asked.

"The paramedics are with her now." Brynn refused to think the worst. "Dad didn't give any other details. He just said to come as fast as I can."

To quell her reaction to the terrible news, Brynn took a deep breath, blew it out and focused hard to allow her training to kick in. The most difficult part of her work as a police officer was suppressing her feelings when tragedy struck. She knew everyone in the valley, and they were all like family. When a crime was committed, she took it personally. But emotions clouded judgment, and she couldn't do her job if she wasn't thinking clearly.

"What kind of attack?" Rand asked.

Brynn shook her head. "Daddy didn't say. Just

that someone had broken in and attacked Mrs. Bick-erstaff. We'll know soon enough."

She was glad she didn't have to urge Rand to hurry. If he went any faster, even the road-hugging Jag would never make the sharp curves. Questions ricocheted through her mind like a frightened bird in a too-small cage. Was Mrs. Bickerstaff all right? Who would have done this to her? And why?

With the questions, ugly suspicions raised their heads. Vandals? Drug addicts stealing objects to fence for their next fix? Or, the most insidious pos-sibility of all, someone who wanted the old woman to feel unsafe in her lifelong home? Someone who intended to frighten Mrs. Bickerstaff so badly she would agree to sell the farm she loved?

Please, God, not the latter, Brynn prayed. Bad enough that she suspected Rand of underhanded business dealings, but she wouldn't believe he'd place an old woman's life at risk for his own profit. Not the Rand she'd grown to love.

There had to be another motive.

The drive to Blackberry Farm took only twenty tense, silent minutes, but to Brynn, it seemed like hours. Rand, concentrating on the road, said noth-ing, and she was afraid to speak, fearful she'd put her horrible suspicions into words.

When the Jaguar pulled up in front of the farm-house, Rand parked between a Pleasant Valley pa-trol car and an ambulance. Brynn's heart hammered in her throat. The fact that the ambulance was still there meant either Mrs. Bickerstaff's injuries weren't life threatening, or—

Brynn shoved the morbid thought away, wrenched opened the car door and took the porch steps two at a time. Rand followed.

Lucas Rhodes met them in the front hall, his handsome face grim, anger flashing in his eyes.

"How is she?" Brynn asked.

"Better than you'd expect. Your father's with her." Lucas glanced over her shoulder at Rand. "You must be Benedict."

Rand offered his hand. "Call me Rand. Any idea who did this?"

Lucas set his mouth in a tight line and jerked his head toward the front parlor. "You'll have to ask the chief."

Brynn brushed past Lucas and entered the parlor with Rand close behind. A quick survey of the room revealed the chaos the intruders had created. Drawers were flung open, their contents strewn. Pillows had been tossed from chairs and sofas, books raked from their shelves onto the floor, curtains yanked from their rods. Mrs. Bickerstaff sat in her favorite rocker with Brynn's father in a chair drawn beside hers. Although the old woman's hands trembled, she greeted Brynn with a reassuring smile that loosened the anxiety in her chest. Two paramedics with a stretcher hovered on the other side of the room.

"What happened?" Brynn asked.

"I'm not sure," Mrs. Bickerstaff said. "One minute I was sound asleep. The next thing I knew, someone was tying my hands and feet while another person was rummaging through the bureau and closet in my bedroom. I tried to fight him off, but he was too strong."

Brynn noted a bruise on the old woman's cheek and tamped down the anger that threatened to strangle her. "Did they hurt you?"

"Other than scaring the living daylights out of me?" Eileen shook her head. "Just a few bruises. Once they left, however, I was afraid I might die before anyone found me. Luckily, I was finally able to loosen the cords on my hands and reach my bedside phone to call for help."

Brynn tried not to think of the hours that the woman had lain helpless, frightened and alone.

"Why, Rand—" Mrs. Bickerstaff greeted him with a fond smile. "I didn't know you were here, too."

"Glad to see you're unhurt," Rand said with feeling, "and I'd like to get my hands on whoever did this."

"Did you recognize anyone?" Brynn asked her.

Mrs. Bickerstaff shook her head. "It was too dark to see their faces. But they were young men. Their voices weren't familiar, but they called each other Daniel and Josh. And they kept hurrying each other, saying they had to get back to the farm before they were missed."

Brynn met her father's gaze and knew they were

both thinking of Jeff's at-risk teens, Daniel and Josh, who lived at Archer Farm.

"Anything stolen?" Brynn asked.

"I haven't had a chance to search." The old woman cast a scolding glance at Brynn's father. "Hunt is treating me like an invalid. But a cursory glance tells me my purse and computer are missing."

"Find any physical evidence?" Brynn asked her father.

He shook his head. "Nothing useful. We've dusted for prints, but Eileen says they were wearing gloves when they tied her up, so I doubt we'll find any."

"That's strange," Rand said. "Why would they wear gloves but call each other by name?"

Brynn shoved aside the chilling thought that the pair might not have expected Mrs. Bickerstaff to survive to identify them.

Lucas had entered the room. "We did find one item that doesn't belong to Mrs. Bickerstaff." He handed Brynn a clear plastic evidence bag that held a silver earring shaped like a skull.

Brynn examined the earring and frowned. "The Josh and Daniel I know don't wear jewelry."

"You know these men?" Rand's outrage at the intruders seemed as deep and genuine as her own.

"I know *a* Josh and *a* Daniel. They're two of Jeff's boys at Archer Farm. But I can't believe they're involved. If you'll take me home, please, I'll get my car and question them."

"I'll take you to the farm," Rand volunteered.

Brynn struggled with her emotions—a jumble of anger at what Mrs. Bickerstaff had suffered, regret at the involvement of two of her favorite boys and puzzlement over how much, if any, Rand was involved in the terrible events at Blackberry Farm. Already overwhelmed, she didn't have the emotional strength to deal further today with Rand or her feelings for him. She'd have to face both later.

"I'd better go alone."

"Suit yourself," Rand said easily, "but I can't allow you to question them without my presence."

"You have something to do with this?" her father demanded.

Rand shook his head. "I'm providing legal counsel for Archer Farm. These boys are in a precarious position. They deserve a lawyer."

Brynn rolled her eyes heavenward. Lordy, she would have to deal with Rand after all. "Then let's get going. The sooner they're questioned, the better."

Rand knelt in front of Mrs. Bickerstaff and took her hands. "Why don't you come to River Walk until we get this sorted out? Or at least until someone can clean up the mess these vandals made. Lillian and I will take good care of you."

"You're a sweet man, Rand Benedict," Eileen said with a smile that placed the old sparkle back in her gray eyes, "no matter what they say about you," she added with a widening of her grin.

"She's going to the hospital first," the chief said.

"No need for that," Eileen insisted. "I'm perfectly fine."

Hunt's face took on an intractable look that barred further discussion. "We'll let Dr. Anderson be the judge of how fine you are. When he says you're okay, you can decide where you want to be."

Rand patted the old woman's hands and stood. "Just remember my invitation. You're always welcome at River Walk."

Rand stepped aside for the paramedics to place Mrs. Bickerstaff on the stretcher and roll it out to the waiting ambulance. Worry clouded his eyes and created a furrow between his brows, reminding Brynn of the way he'd looked the night he drove Jared to the hospital. Rand seemed genuinely concerned for the old woman. He never would have knowingly placed her in danger—but Brynn couldn't be certain of anything now.

"Lucas and I will finish up here," her father told her. "You let Mr. Benedict take you to the farm." The slightest lift of his eyebrows reminded her of her earlier assignment, to keep tabs on Rand. "Let me know what you find out," he added with double meaning.

Rand extended his hand to her father. "Sorry we had to meet under such circumstances, Chief Sawyer. I hope the next time will be better."

"So do I." Her father shook Rand's hand and raked him with a piercing gaze.

Brynn suppressed a groan. Rand's meeting her father wasn't anything like she'd once envisioned. Not that her father's approval was a factor now. She could tell by the look in his eyes that he had serious doubts about Rand. Doubts Brynn couldn't help but share, until she could prove otherwise.

With a sigh, she headed toward Rand's car once more, recalling a phrase Eileen had once forwarded her from a Web chat room: if the world didn't suck, we'd all fall off.

"STOP THE CAR!" Brynn demanded as soon as Rand had turned off the highway onto the Archer Farm drive.

She'd been strangely quiet since leaving Mrs. Bickerstaff's place, and Rand, thinking she was planning her interrogation of Josh and Daniel, hadn't interrupted her thoughts. Her sudden explosion caught him by surprise.

Rand slammed on the brakes and turned to face her. "What's wrong? You forget something?"

Brynn wrenched open the door, hopped from the car and stalked a few yards up the road.

Puzzled, Rand climbed out and followed. The noon sun flooded the drive with light and glistened off the dark green leaves of rhododendron. Birds flitted through the trees, and in the distance, he could detect the soothing trickle of a stream gurgling down the mountain. Brynn's stiff posture and the turmoil of emotions on her face were at sharp odds with the tranquil surroundings.

Rand approached her, and she whirled on him, eyes blazing. "I want the truth," she demanded, "and I want it now."

He craved to reach for her, to hold her close, but with her attitude as prickly as a thorn hedge, he kept his hands to himself and attempted to gentle her with his voice. "The truth is that I love you, Brynn."

For a moment, she looked as if she'd been sucker-punched, but she soon found her breath. "Then why have you lied to me?"

"I haven't lied."

"You didn't come to the valley to buy land for Farrington Properties?" Anger sparked like deep blue flames in her magnificent eyes, and she clenched her slender fingers at her sides.

Regret scorched his gut. Her knowledge of his connection with Farrington explained her current rage, and he wished he'd had a chance to explain the situation himself. She'd jumped to the wrong conclusions and believed him guilty of lies of omission, apparently among other things, judging from the ferocity of her reaction.

"I don't deny that I was working as Farrington's agent. But I haven't broken any laws."

"What about the laws of common decency?" Her low voice shook with emotion.

"I should have told you—"

"That's not what I mean," she snapped.

He struggled for calm and fought against the horrible sensation that he was watching the prospects for his perfect future crumble before his eyes. "I'm not a mind reader. You'll have to fill me in."

She flung her arm toward the direction from which they'd come. "This entire break-in scheme at Mrs. Bickerstaff's stinks to high heaven."

"I couldn't agree more." He knotted his forehead in concentration, trying to follow her reasoning, or lack thereof.

"There were valuables strewn all over that farmhouse, from silver candlesticks to antique clocks and solid gold jewelry, items a real burglar would have taken in a heartbeat, especially when he had all night to gather his loot, but none of them were touched."

"Go on," Rand said with a sinking heart. "I'm listening."

She paced the road in front of him, grinding the gravel beneath her feet before she confronted him again. "Did you ask Mrs. Bickerstaff to sell her farm to Farrington?"

The ugliness of her suspicions hit him, and with it came a surge of anger. "What are you implying?"

"Just answer my question!" Her voice had risen an octave, her face was flushed and her fists were clenched.

"Yes, I asked her, before she told me what she wanted in her will."

"And Eileen refused to sell?"

"Why ask if you already know the answer?"

"Because I'm trying to make sense of this whole horrible mess." Her full lower lip trembled slightly, a hint at the distress hovering beneath her rage.

He kept his voice low in hopes of soothing Brynn's escalating temper and putting a lid on his own. "The break-in at Blackberry Farm was a senseless act of violence. You can't attach meaning to something like that."

"Oh, there's meaning there, all right." Her voice was harsh, and her words struck him like hard-thrown rocks. She stopped pacing and crossed her arms over her chest. "And apparently there's intent, as well."

"What kind of intent?" His own anger threatened to break lose from his restraint, and, if it did, they were both lost.

"What if—" Brynn skewered him with a narrowed gaze and cold eyes. "What if someone decided to *make* Eileen want to sell?"

Her accusation brought Rand up short, forced him to consider possibilities he hadn't faced. When he had first met Farrington, he'd sensed an undercurrent of ruthlessness in the man. How far was the developer willing to go to insure a generous profit? Far enough to break not only the civil statutes but the laws of human decency, as well? Rand wasn't sure how ruthless Farrington was, but he could quote plenty of case law where men had committed much worse deeds for less.

He turned Brynn's question back on her. "What makes you so sure the break-in isn't exactly what it seems?"

"Because of the valuables left behind. Because, of all the boys at Archer Farm, Daniel and Josh are the *least* likely to be involved in something like this. They're also the only boys from the farm who work in town and whose names are known to almost everyone. Sounds like the intruders were trying *intentionally* to cast blame on Jeff's boys."

Rand nodded. "I agree. I've already said it didn't make sense that the robbers called each other by name in front of Mrs. Bickerstaff."

Brynn set her mouth in a grim line. "What better way to scare an old woman out of her home than to make her think the boys at the adjacent farm are dangerous, a personal threat?"

Rand raked his hand through his hair. "I can't believe Farrington would stoop that low."

"The depths of human depravity ceased to amaze me long ago," Brynn said heatedly.

Rand winced, believing she'd lumped him into the same class as Farrington. "You're jumping to conclusions, officer. Everyone's innocent until proven guilty."

Brynn spun on her heel and headed back to the car. "And that's exactly what I intend to do. I'm going to clear Josh and Daniel, then find who's really responsible for scaring an old woman almost to death."

Knowing she somehow blamed him for what had happened at Blackberry Farm, Rand followed her to the car. He had some proving of his own to do.

Chapter Thirteen

Brynn sat in the farmhouse kitchen with Daniel and Josh across the table from her. Rand sat between them, and Jeff leaned against the kitchen counter, powerful arms crossed over his broad chest, his expression grim. Never had Brynn felt so personally involved in an investigation. In addition to her friendship with Jeff and her affection for Daniel and Josh, she had her feelings for Rand to contend with.

In her heart, she believed he'd had nothing to do with the attack on Mrs. Bickerstaff. He'd been as outraged as she was by the senseless violence against a helpless woman. But his lack of participation in that crime didn't absolve him from his underhanded method of trying to buy land without telling her. Just moments earlier, at the foot of the drive, he'd said he loved her. But if he loved her, he wouldn't have hidden the reason he'd come to the valley. And if he'd kept that fact secret, had anything he'd told her been the truth? She thrust aside that burning question to concentrate on the task at hand.

She'd allowed Rand time alone with the boys before questioning them, since she was already convinced of their innocence. Her interrogation was only a matter of procedure. Her instincts, operating at full throttle, informed her that the lawbreakers were nowhere near Archer Farm.

"I have just a few questions," she began, glancing first at Daniel, then Josh.

The boys both looked to Rand, who nodded. "Tell Officer Sawyer whatever she wants to know."

Daniel swallowed hard and his large Adam's apple bobbed in his thin neck. Jason, short and built like a fire hydrant, sat stoically without moving.

"Where were you last night, Daniel?" she asked.

"Asleep in my dorm room." His voice broke with nervousness. "We turned in at eleven o'clock after watching a DVD of *The Day After Tomorrow.*"

"And you, Josh?"

The stocky teen set his jaw in a hard line, more, Brynn realized to keep from trembling than from obstinance. "I share a room with Daniel, Tyrone and Cooper. We were all there from lights out till reveille this morning."

"I questioned Cooper and Tyrone," Jeff said, "and they corroborate Josh and Daniel's alibi." He gave a shrug of his shoulders.

Brynn knew what Jeff was thinking. The counselors at the farm had worked wonders with the boys, but the code of the street still ran deep. Snitching on one's friends wasn't acceptable, so Cooper's and Tyrone's statements had to be taken with a grain of salt.

"Either of you boys ever been to Blackberry Farm?" Brynn continued.

"Not me," Josh insisted. "Just seen the sign passing by."

Daniel shook his head.

"Either of you have anything you want to tell me?" Brynn asked.

"What's this about, Officer Sawyer?" Daniel asked. "Are we in trouble?"

Brynn smiled, the first she'd allowed herself since the boys had entered the kitchen. "I don't think so, Daniel. I just have some loose ends to tie up."

"Anything else you want to ask my clients?" Rand said.

Brynn shook her head.

"You can go," Jeff told the boys. "And Daniel, maybe you'd better take a few days off from work at the café until Officer Sawyer finishes her investigation."

At Daniel's crestfallen expression, new anger at the perpetrators of the crime flooded Brynn. Daniel had been falsely accused once before, when Jodie's cook had borrowed money from the till to pay her daughter's medical bills. It seemed as if the harder the kid tried to turn his life around, the more punches fate threw at him.

"It'll be okay, Daniel," Brynn assured him. "I promise you."

"Then why do I need a lawyer?" Daniel asked.

"I'm your guarantee that you're going to be okay," Rand said quickly.

Brynn repressed a sigh of frustration. Rand had said exactly the right words to reassure the boys, his voice filled with genuine concern. How could a man of such obvious good intentions be the same man who had misled her so badly?

Apparently unconvinced by Rand's assurances, Daniel nodded nervously to Rand and followed Josh out the back door.

As the boys were leaving, Gofer entered from the front hall. "The staff has finished its search of all the buildings and grounds. We've even combed the surrounding woods. No sign of Mrs. Bickerstaff's computer or purse."

Brynn raised an eyebrow. "That was fast."

"Chief Sawyer called before you arrived," Gofer explained, "so we had a head start."

He removed from his shirt pocket the plastic evidence bag with the skull earring that Brynn had loaned him earlier and placed it on the table in front of her. "I also went through the boys' belongings that we took from them when they first arrived here. No such animal as this earring listed there." He paused for a moment. "I guess, though, there's always the possibility Josh or Daniel could have bought it in town."

"Where?" Brynn asked with a snort of surprise. "Not at Fulton's Department Store, that's for sure."

"Maybe at one of the booths at Daffodil Days?" Jeff asked with a worried look. "They were both working in town that day."

Rand shook his head. "I didn't see anyone selling this kind of jewelry."

"Me, either," Brynn said, "and I spent a lot of hours inspecting every vendor's table."

At the sound of running footsteps in the hall, all four adults looked to the door. Brittany, Jodie's teenage daughter, pale blond hair flying, face flushed and green eyes dark with anger, burst into the room.

"You can't arrest Daniel, Aunt Brynn," the teen said heatedly. "He hasn't done anything."

Brynn recalled that Daniel and Brittany had been tight since their first meeting a year ago. Working together at the café, they had grown even closer.

"Cool your jets, Brit," Jeff said calmly. "Brynn is here to clear Daniel's name, not to take him in."

Brittany looked from her stepfather to Brynn, and the tension left her body. Then her gaze fell on Rand. "Who are you?"

"Rand Benedict. I live at River Walk. Nice to finally meet you, Brittany."

Brittany flopped into the chair beside him. "Mom's told me about you." Her pretty face wrinkled in a mischievous grin. "And Aunt Brynn."

Rand shot Brynn an amused glance, which she ignored, before he turned back to Brittany. "I'd be interested in what your mother's told you."

"Well—" Brittany began, then caught sight of the evidence bag on the table. She grabbed it and held it up to the light. "Cool."

Brynn noted the three earrings in each of Brittany's ears and recalled the battle Jodie had won, drawing the line at further body piercings. Since Jeff had come into Jodie and Brit's lives, the teen had gradually shed her walking-dead Goth look, but she retained her love of jewelry.

"Ever seen anything like this before?" Brynn kept her voice casual.

"Not for a couple years," Brit said. "But Skeeter Welch wore this kind of stuff all the time."

"Who's Skeeter Welch?" Rand said.

Pieces of the puzzle were finally coming together for Brynn. "Skeeter's a kid from Carsons Corner. Has several priors. Runs with a bad crowd."

She omitted the fact that Brittany had hung with that crowd, too, during her ultrarebellious stage, before her mother had taken her for serious counseling.

"Is Skeeter in trouble?" Brittany asked.

"Don't know yet," Brynn said. "I'll have to question him."

Brittany rose from her chair and grabbed cookies from a plate on the counter. "Better Skeeter than Daniel. That dude deserves to be arrested."

Without a backward look, Brit, chewing on a cookie, left the room.

"What's next?" Jeff asked.

Brynn stood and tucked the earring into the pocket of her skirt. "Lucas Rhodes and I are going to pay a visit to Skeeter Welch."

Rand stood also. "I'll drive you back."

Brynn shook her head. She could concentrate on only one problem at a time. The less she was around Rand for now, the better. "I'm sure Jodie will be glad to take me home."

JODIE'S VAN sped along Valley Road toward town. Brynn spent the greater part of the journey filling in Jodie on the break-in at Blackberry Farm. When she'd finished, she added what she'd learned about Rand's reason for coming to Pleasant Valley.

"He lied to me, Jodie," Brynn said when she'd completed her explanation, the full weight of her disappointment pressing on her as if someone had loaded a pallet of bricks on her heart. "He's not on sabbatical. He came here to buy land for his client. And as soon as he's accomplished that, he'll head back to New York and his cushy job at his prestigious law firm." She slammed her fists against her knees. "I knew I should never have trusted a Yankee lawyer."

Jodie snapped her a quick glance before returning her eyes to the road. "He didn't tell you?"

"Tell me what?"

"That he resigned from his law firm."

Surprise stole Brynn's breath. "What?"

Jodie nodded. "Last Friday."

"How come you know this and I don't?" Wounded pride joined Brynn's flood of emotions.

"Rand met me at the café Friday. I took him upstairs to show him our old apartment. He signed a five-year lease on the spot."

Brynn's mouth fell open, but she was at a loss for words.

"He said he'd already quit his job in New York," Jodie continued, "and was opening his own law practice in Pleasant Valley."

"A five-year lease?"

Jodie nodded.

"But he didn't tell me." Why would Rand share his plans with Jodie and not with her? That cut deep.

Jodie reached over and squeezed her hand. "Where were you headed when you got the call about Mrs. Bickerstaff?"

"To the mountains for lunch."

Jodie nodded. "To a romantic inn. Rand asked me about the place. I told him it was a perfect setting."

"Perfect for what?" Brynn's mouth went dry.

"Rand asked me not to tell you about his decision to stay in the valley. He wanted to inform you himself. At lunch today."

Brynn groaned and scooted lower in her seat.

"He didn't actually say," Jodie went on, "but I'm willing to bet that wasn't all he was going to tell you. Or maybe I should say, *ask* you."

"Ask me? What are you talking about?"

Jodie's grin showed her pretty teeth. "The big question."

"Who I voted for in the last election?"

Her friend swatted her playfully on her shoulder. "Are you ever serious?"

"You don't call presidential politics serious?" Brynn hedged, still trying to wrap her mind around the implications of what Jodie had revealed.

"Will you stop joking?" Jodie said.

"I don't approve of political jokes," Brynn shot back. "Too many of them get elected." She used humor to shield her emotions from overload.

Jodie laughed, then her expression sobered. "Rand loves you, Brynn. I can see it in his face, hear it in his voice when he talks about you."

Brynn groaned. "Not anymore."

"What are you saying?"

"I blew up at him this morning. Accused him of lying to me. Pretty much implied that he was responsible for what had happened to Eileen."

"You didn't!" Jodie stared at her in horror, an apt reflection of Brynn's own feelings.

"Keep your eyes on the road," Brynn warned, "or all our problems are over."

Jodie faced forward in time to maneuver an upcoming curve. "What are you going to do?"

"Besides wishing I could start the past month over?"

"Besides that." Jodie's horrified expression morphed into an understanding smile.

Brynn leaned back against the headrest and closed her eyes. "I have absolutely no idea."

JUST OVER a week later, Brynn sat in a redwood lounge chair at the far end of her backyard in the shade of the persimmon tree and watched her father spread compost over the summer perennial beds. The spring day was glorious, filled with cheery sunshine, the scent of flowers and moist earth and the melodies of birdsong, but not even the day's perfection could alleviate Brynn's misery.

Her father stopped his work and leaned on his shovel. He removed a bandanna from the pocket of his dungarees, mopped his forehead, and studied her with a worried frown. "Penny for your thoughts, pumpkin."

Brynn plucked a few blades of the blue fescue lawn that her father tended so carefully and shredded them between her fingers. "I really messed up, Dad."

He propped the shovel against the wheelbarrow, ambled to her chair and sat at her feet. "You solved the Bickerstaff break-in in record time. That doesn't seem like messing up to me."

Brynn tossed the bits of grass aside. "I'm not talking about work."

Her father rubbed his chin with his big hand and

stared back toward the house. "Then you must be talking about Rand Benedict."

She nodded. "I jumped to conclusions. Said terrible things to him. Now I don't know how to take them back."

He patted her knee. "Don't be too hard on yourself. After all, the man did come here under false pretenses."

"But that's just it," Brynn protested. "He came intending to buy property on the sly, but he didn't go through with it."

"Hummph," Hunt said, obviously unconvinced. "Only because Mrs. Bickerstaff and the Mauneys wouldn't sell."

"It wasn't like that. I talked to them. Mrs. Bickerstaff said Rand asked only once if she was interested in selling, but when she told him she had other plans for the property, he backed off. He even expressed approval of her long-range goals for her place."

"And the Mauneys?"

"According to Joe and Vera, Rand never even asked. He alluded to how much they might make if they were to sell, but when they showed no interest, he dropped the subject."

Her father thought for a moment. "Doesn't sound like his heart was in his work."

Brynn had drawn the same conclusion. "That's just it, Daddy. I think Rand's heart is in the valley. That's why he quit his job—and why he wants to stay."

"And what does his staying have to do with you?"

"Nothing now," Brynn said miserably. "I've ruined my chances."

"Have you told him you're sorry?" her father asked gently. "And admitted that you were wrong about him?"

Brynn shook her head. She hadn't heard a word from Rand since she left Archer Farm with Jodie more than a week ago. After the terrible things she'd said, and the even worse things she'd implied, she didn't blame him for not speaking to her. He'd probably never speak to her again. *Ever.*

"I don't think an apology will do any good," she said, wishing she could take her father's shovel, dig a hole and disappear into it.

Her father patted her knee. "You won't know unless you try. Besides, what's the worst thing that could happen if you tell him you're sorry? I did tell you to keep an eye on him."

"He might say he'd never want to see me again." The prospect lodged a boulder-sized lump in her throat.

"And is he seeing you now?"

She shook her head.

"Then what do you have to lose?" Hunt patted her knee again and stood. "From the way I figure it, an apology might help, and it sure won't hurt. I'm headed to the builders' supply. You think about what I've said."

Her father crossed the yard, climbed into his pickup and backed out the drive.

Brynn mulled over his advice. In her entire life, her father had never steered her wrong. But how did she go about apologizing? A phone call wouldn't do it. She could articulate what she needed to say, but she couldn't watch Rand to gauge his reaction. And if she went to River Walk, would he let her in? He had Lillian to run interference if he didn't want to talk to Brynn. She could lie in wait in her patrol car on Valley Road and pull him over, she thought with a fleeting smile—but such an encounter wouldn't set the proper tone for reconciliation.

Her head pounded from thinking too hard. Hoping to ease its ache, she leaned back in the chair and closed her eyes. The warm breeze and peaceful surroundings soon lulled her to sleep.

WHEN BRYNN opened her eyes, she thought she was dreaming. Rand sat in the chair next to hers, his steady gaze focused on her face. With the breeze ruffling his thick hair and the dappled sunlight highlighting the rugged angles of his face, he looked like a dream model for L.L.Bean in tan chinos, a pale yellow shirt and cordovan deck shoes. Too handsome to be true. She had to be dreaming. She blinked and looked again.

He was still there.

She struggled upright and quickly rubbed the back of her hand across her lips, hoping she hadn't drooled in her sleep. Happiness at the sight of him shot through her like a bottle rocket. "Why didn't you wake me?"

"You've had a tough week." His voice caressed her, and his eyes lighted with a tender smile. "I thought you needed the rest."

Sitting up straighter, she adjusted her shirt and cursed the fact that for what might be the most important conversation in her life, she was dressed in old jeans and a grass-stained T-shirt she'd donned to work in the yard with her dad.

"You've been busy, too, I hear." She resisted the impulse to finger-comb her hair. "Mrs. Bickerstaff told me how you cleaned up the mess Skeeter Welch and his crony made of her house that night."

"Eileen refused to stay overnight at the hospital for observation. And she wouldn't come to River Walk. All she wanted was to go home." He shrugged. "I couldn't let her go back to that chaos."

Her heart hammered against her rib cage. She couldn't believe they were sitting in her own backyard having a perfectly ordinary conversation, when all she craved was to throw her arms around Rand and beg him to forgive her for having been so judgmental. But the last thing she wanted was to scare him away before she apologized properly, so she clasped her hands in her lap and waited for the right opportunity.

"I spoke with Eileen a few days ago," Brynn said, surprised her voice sounded normal when her pulse was pounding like a heavy metal band's drummer on speed. "She seems fully recovered."

Rand nodded and leaned back in his chair. For several minutes they said nothing. Enjoying the silence like an old married couple, she thought, pleased with the comparison. The outdoor sounds swirled around them with the breeze, a peaceful counterpoint to Brynn's inner turmoil.

"I was going—" she began.

"I wanted—" he said at the same time.

They both stopped speaking.

"You first," Rand said with a nod.

"I was planning to come see you later this afternoon," she said.

"Official business?"

She shook her head, then corrected herself. "Well, partly. I wanted to let you know that we've caught Skeeter Welch and Jay Kraft. But I suppose the valley gossips have filled you in on their arrest by now."

He leaned toward her and clasped his hands between his knees. A dozen memories and as many fantasies about those marvelous hands flitted through her mind, and she struggled to concentrate on his words. "You know how gossip is," he said. "Tell me what really happened."

Brynn relaxed slightly. She was on safer ground talking about her work. "On the tip from Brittany about the earring, Lucas and I drove to Skeeter Welch's house near Carsons Corner. Skeeter answered the door, wearing the matching skull earring in his left ear. We asked if we could come in and talk to him."

"He let you in?" Rand looked surprised.

"Skeeter's not the brightest bulb in the chandelier," Brynn said. "And his even dimmer sidekick, Jay, was sitting in the living room, drinking beer. Eileen's computer was sitting on the dining room table in plain view."

Rand raised his eyebrows. "How did you know it was hers?"

"It still had her password taped to the front in large letters. I used to warn her about displaying it, but she insisted having it there saved her time from trying to remember it."

"And that was it? Case closed?"

Brynn grinned. "We arrested Dumb and Dumber and headed back to the station. Halfway into town, Skeeter was sobbing his eyes out, wanting to cut a deal." She hesitated, knowing she was back on dangerous ground.

"What kind of deal?"

"Said he'd give us the name of the guy who'd hired them to scare Mrs. Bickerstaff if we'd cut them some slack."

"But the name the man gave Skeeter was fake," Rand said.

Brynn jerked her head up in astonishment. "How did you know?"

"Because I've been doing some investigating on

my own." He reached into the pocket of his slacks, withdrew a paper and handed it to her.

She unfolded it and saw immediately the gold-embossed letterhead of Steinman, Slagle and Crump. After scanning the contents quickly, she gazed at Rand in disbelief. "You found him?"

"Not me personally," Rand said with a self-deprecating look. "But Charles Steinman has the best in-house team of private investigators in New York. When I informed him that Gus Farrington might be using strong-arm tactics to force land sales, Steinman put his P.I.s to work. It didn't take them long to track down Farrington's henchman. He's cooling his heels in a New York jail now, awaiting extradition, if you want him."

Brynn remembered the bruise on Mrs. Bicker-staff's cheek and the shambles the intruders had made of the old woman's house. "I want him, all right."

"I was hoping you'd say that," Rand said.

"And Farrington?"

"Steinman will bring down the full force of the law on Farrington." Rand looked so fierce, Brynn shivered. She never wanted to see him that angry at her. Then his expression softened. "Charles is competitive, even cutthroat when it comes to business, but he's not dishonest. He's as outraged and disgusted about Farrington's tactics as we are."

Brynn summoned her courage, took a deep breath and plunged. "That brings me to the other reason I was coming to see you. I want to apologize."

He shook his head. "You don't owe me an apology."

"But I do. I assumed that you'd come to the valley to buy land secretly—"

"I did," Rand said bluntly.

"But you didn't go through with it," she insisted.

He took her hands in his and met her gaze without flinching. "I came with every intention of gobbling up acreage for Gus Farrington before the good folks of Pleasant Valley knew what hit them."

"What changed your mind?" Emotion tightened her chest, making her voice a breathless whisper.

"You did." He curved his lips in a heart-stopping smile and tightened his grip on her hands. "You and the valley worked your magic. I didn't want to spoil this place for you or any of the people who've opened their homes and hearts to me. That's why I resigned from the law firm. Why I rented office space from Jodie. I want Pleasant Valley to be my home, too."

She had to be dreaming. Had her Yankee lawyer just declared he loved the valley as much as she did? "Can you forgive me for saying such awful things to you?"

"You were defending the people you love."

"And you're one of them," she said quietly. "I love you, Rand. And I'll never question your integrity again."

He stood, pulled her to her feet and wrapped his

arms around her. His body felt solid, warm and right against hers.

"That brings up another question," he said.

She pressed her cheek against his heart and heard the thunder of its beating. "Ask anything you like."

With gentle fingers, he lifted her chin until their eyes met. "Will you marry me, Brynn?"

Words failed her and tears of happiness filled her eyes.

"And Jared, too," he added. "We come as a package deal."

"Lordy," she said with a sigh, "a woman would have to be crazy to turn down a package like that."

He pulled her closer. "Is that a yes?"

She tilted her head and studied him, working hard to keep the mischief from her expression. "I've been more than a little crazy lately."

His face clouded with disappointment.

"Crazy in love," she amended, throwing her arms around his neck. "Yes, I'll marry you."

With a whoop, he picked her off her feet and whirled her in a circle before kissing her, an embrace that threatened to steal all the oxygen from her body and consume her like a flame.

She finally pulled away for air, just as her dad climbed out of his pickup in front of the garage. Hunt's smile was wider than the valley. "Glad to see you two have worked things out."

"We're getting married, Dad," Brynn said.

Hunt's gaze flickered over the flower-filled backyard and his eyes glazed briefly with memory before he held out his hand and shook Rand's firmly. His earlier reservations about the man were forgotten. "Marriage is a good thing. Welcome to the family, son."

Epilogue

An early autumn frost had worked its magic on the valley, turning the poplars a sunny yellow and the maples into breathtaking spectacles of gold and red. Only the majestic oaks maintained a vestige of deep green. At makeshift stands along Valley Road, farmers stacked pumpkins, bundles of colorful Indian corn and baskets of apples to entice tourists on their way to the mountains to view the fall colors.

In town, the maples that lined Piedmont Avenue were a flamboyant display of color, echoed by a rainbow of chrysanthemums in pots and window boxes in front of the shops.

And Hunt Sawyer's backyard was a gardener's delight, its verdant green lawn edged with beds of bronze and gold chrysanthemums, deep purple dahlias and autumn sedum. At the far end, beneath the persimmon tree, a trellis, covered with English ivy, had been erected. Standing in front of the trellis with Judge Byrd, his mentor from law school who would perform the wedding ceremony, Rand looked over the guests who'd assembled in the folding chairs.

With Mrs. Bickerstaff, Lillian, the Mauneys, Bud and Marion Sawyer, the Fultons and the staff and boys of Archer Farm were many others who were not only friends but now clients, too. Since opening his office last spring, Rand had been both amazed and gratified at the number of people in the valley who had requested his services. He'd helped with wills, trusts, business contracts, real estate sales and even a restraining order and divorce proceedings for a woman who'd suffered domestic abuse. He'd found the work surprisingly rewarding, much more so than any corporate deal he'd ever closed. And he'd even made new friends in the process—not something that had ever happened in New York.

He looked toward the back of the house, hoping for a glimpse of Brynn, but the wedding party was still inside. No one seemed in a hurry except him. The guests were chatting quietly among themselves while the string quartet he'd imported from Greenville played music that Brynn had selected, unfamiliar tunes with a happy beat that for once didn't make him feel depressed.

Nearer the house, the catering staff was putting the last touches on the linen-draped buffet tables, and Rand spotted Jared, poking a finger into the icing of the wedding cake before Jodie whisked the boy back inside.

This time last year, Rand recalled, he'd feared Jared would never smile again. But the intervening months with all their blessings had worked wonders on the boy, who was as much in love with the woman he called "Mama Bwynn" as Rand was.

"I'm going to quit my job as soon as we're married," Brynn had told Rand.

"Are you sure?" He knew how much she enjoyed police work.

"Absolutely. Lillian is wonderful, but Jared needs a mother." Her dark blue eyes sparkled. "And a baby sister or brother. I can always go back to work once the children are in school."

Rand couldn't believe his good fortune. Formerly a lone wolf—a predatory legal one at that—he now had family, friends and a warm, supportive community who more than made up for the fact that his elitist parents had declined to make the trip from Paris for the wedding. The flutter of excitement in his stomach reminded him how long it had been since he'd needed the antacids he'd lived on for so many years in his high-pressure job in the city.

The string quartet and the guests fell silent, and the only sound was the breeze rustling the dry leaves of the surrounding trees and scattering the waiting crowd with fluttering bits of red and gold. The musicians struck the first chord of the wedding march, and the guests rose to their feet.

Jared came down the white carpeted aisle first,

carrying a satin pillow with the matching yellow-gold wedding rings. Rand could detect the tip of the boy's tongue, tucked in the corner of his lips, as Jared concentrated on navigating the distance between the house and the trellis. Even though the rings were lightly tacked to the pillow, Jared had been worried that they might fall off in transit. When he reached the trellis, Rand grasped the boy's shoulder and gave him a smile of approval.

Brittany, on Daniel's arm, was next down the aisle. When Brynn had suggested that Daniel escort her goddaughter, Rand had applauded the idea. What better way to show the community their love and respect for the teenager who'd suffered twice from false allegations since his arrival in the valley?

Brittany and Daniel were followed by Jodie and Jeff, then Grant and Merrilee. The men's tuxedoes matched Rand's and the women wore elegant gowns of russet taffeta that changed colors from bronze to gold as they moved, reminding Rand of the highlights in Brynn's hair.

The music swelled, and Brynn started down the aisle with her arm through her father's. Rand's breath caught in his throat. Foregoing traditional bridal white, Brynn had chosen a gown the color of pale champagne that complemented her creamy skin and thick auburn hair, upswept with soft, dangling curls that framed her face.

At that moment, her gaze met his, and he remembered nothing else throughout the ceremony except the love shining in those eyes. And the first kiss as husband and wife, of course.

The wedding dinner was also a blur filled with smiling faces, warm wishes and congratulatory toasts. After the cake had been cut and the champagne poured, Grant clinked his spoon against his glass. "I think it's time we heard from the groom," he said when the guests had quieted.

Brynn leaned toward Rand, kissed his cheek and said, "Show them what a silver-tongued devil you are."

Rand rose to his feet, lifted his glass and surveyed the crowd with an expectant pause. "Have you heard the one about the Yankee lawyer and the Southern cop?"

The guests, well aware of Brynn's propensity for both lawyer and Yankee jokes, groaned good-naturedly.

"I don't believe I know that one," Brynn said. "How does it go?"

Still unable to believe this gorgeous creature was really his wife, he returned her dazzling smile.

"They met," he said, "they fell in love, they were married surrounded by family and friends—" He gestured to the surrounding group. "And they lived happily ever after."

"Wif me," Jared insisted loudly.

"With their wonderful son, Jared," Rand added with a smile for the boy.

The roar of applause barely registered as Brynn laughed, kissed Rand and whispered in his ear, "This time, looks like the joke's on me."

* * * * *

*Don't miss Charlotte Douglas's next book
in Harlequin Intrigue,
MYSTIQUE,
part of the ECLIPSE series,
in June 2005!*

Welcome to the world of American Romance!
Turn the page for excerpts
from our May 2005 titles.

THE RICH BOY by Leah Vale

HIS FAMILY by Muriel Jensen

THE SERGEANT'S BABY by Bonnie Gardner

HOMETOWN HONEY by Kara Lennox

We're sure you'll enjoy every one of these books!

The Rich Boy (#1065) is the fourth and final book in Leah Vale's popular series THE LOST MILLIONAIRES. The previous titles are *The Bad Boy, The Cowboy* and *The Marine*.

In this book, you'll read about Alexander McCoy. He's just found out that the mighty McCoy family, one of the richest in the nation, has a skeleton in its closet. When reporter Madeline Monroe discovers the secret, she will do anything she can to prove that she's more than just a pretty face. This is a story about two people from very different walks of life, who both want to be loved for *who* they are—not *what* they are.

I, Marcus Malcom McCoy, being of sound mind, yadda yadda yadda, do hereby acknowledge as my biological progeny the firstborn to Helen Metzger, Ann Branigan, Bonnie Larson and Nadine Anders et al, who were paid a million dollars each for their silence. Upon my death and subsequent reading of this addendum to my last will and testament, their children shall inherit equal portions of my estate and, excepting Helen's child, Alexander, who

already has the privilege, shall immediately take their rightful places in the family and family business, whatever it may be at that time.
Marcus M. McCoy

Tuning out the chatter from the party going on the other side of the study's locked doors, Alexander McCoy slumped back in the big desk chair. Staring at the scrawled signature at the bottom of the hand-written page, he tugged loose his black tuxedo's traditional bow tie. If only he could tune out the burn of betrayal as easily.

For what seemed to be the hundredth time, he had to admit to himself that he was definitely looking at the signature of the man he'd spent his life believing to be his brother. The brother he'd initially admired, then set out to be as different from as possible. And only Marcus would have had the nerve to belittle legalities by actually writing *yadda, yadda, yadda* especially on something as important as an addendum to his last will and testament.

Even if Alex could harbor any doubts, he would have had a hard time dismissing the word of David Weidman. The McCoys' longtime family lawyer had witnessed Marcus writing the addendum—though David claimed to have not read the document before sealing it in the heavy cream envelope that bore his signature and noting the existence of the unorthodox addendum in the actual will.

A will that had been read nearly a month ago. Four days after Marcus had been killed on June 8 while fly-fishing in Alaska, by a grizzly bear that hadn't appreciated the competition. Before the reading of the will, Alex had grieved for the relationship he'd hoped to one day finally develop with his much older brother. Now…

Muriel Jensen's *His Family* (#1066) is the third book in her series THE ABBOTTS, about three brothers whose sister was kidnapped when she was fourteen months old. At the end of the second book, *His Wife,* we met China Grant, a woman who thought that she might have been that kidnapped daughter, but as it turns out, she's not. No one is happier about that than Campbell Abbott—who never believed she could be a relation.

Campbell Abbott put an arm around China Grant's shoulders and walked her away from the fairground's picnic table and into the trees. She was sobbing and he didn't know what to do. He wasn't good with women. Well, he was, but not when they were crying.

"I was so *sure!*" she said in a fractured voice.

He squeezed her shoulders. "I know. I'm sorry."

She sobbed, sniffed, then speculated. "I don't suppose DNA tests are ever wrong?"

"I'm certain that's possible," he replied, "but I'm also fairly certain they were particularly careful with this case. Everyone on Long Island is aware that the Abbott's little girl was kidnapped as a toddler. That you might be her returned after twenty-five years had everyone hoping the test would be positive."

"Except you." She'd said it without rancor, and that surprised him. In the month since she'd turned up at Shepherd's Knoll, looking for her family, he'd done his best to make things difficult for her. In the beginning he'd simply doubted her claims, certain any enterprising young woman could buy a toddler's blue corduroy rompers at a used-clothing store and claim she was an Abbott Mills heiress because she had an outfit similar to what the child was wearing when she'd been taken. As he'd told his elder brothers repeatedly, Abbott Mills had made thousands, possibly millions, of those corduroy rompers.

Campbell had wanted her to submit to a DNA test then and there. If she was Abigail, he was her full sibling, and therefore would be a match.

But Chloe, his mother, had been in Paris at the time, caring for a sick aunt, and Killian, his eldest brother, hadn't wanted to upset her further. He'd suggested they wait until Chloe returned home.

Sawyer, his second brother, had agreed. Accustomed to being outvoted by them most of his life, Campbell had accepted his fate when Killian further suggested that China stay on to help Campbell manage the Abbotts' estate until Chloe came home. Killian was CEO of Abbott Mills, and Sawyer headed the Abbott Mills Foundation.

Killian and Sawyer were the products of their father's first marriage to a Texas oil heiress. Campbell and the missing Abigail were born to his second wife, Chloe, a former designer for Abbott Mills.

When Chloe had come back from Paris two weeks ago, the test had been taken immediately. The results had been couriered to the house that afternoon. China had been there alone while everyone else had been preparing for the hospital fund-raiser that had just taken place this afternoon and evening. She'd brought the sealed envelope with her and opened it just moments ago, when the family had been all together at the picnic table.

They'd all expected a very different result.

After spending most of her life as either an army brat or a military wife, Bonnie Gardner knows about men in uniform, and knows their wives, their girlfriends and their mothers. She's been all of them! In her latest book, *The Sergeant's Baby* (#1067), Air Force Technical Sergeant Danny Murphey is in for a big surprise—Allison Raneea Carter is pregnant. With more than a little past history together, Danny has to wonder—is the woman who refused to marry him because she wanted her independence carrying his child? Find out what it's going to take for her to change her mind about marrying him *this* time!

Danny Murphey lay quietly in bed in the darkened hotel room and listened to the soft, rhythmic breathing of the woman beside him. He reached over and caressed the velvety smooth, olive skin of her cheek and was rewarded with a sleepy smile and a soft moan of pleasure. It was music to him after two endless years apart.

He found it hard to believe, after so much time, but Allison Raneea Carter was really here, lying be-

side him, in this bed. She had responded to him—
they had responded to each other as if they were de-
signed to be the other's perfect match. It seemed
almost as if the past two years had never happened.

Technical Sergeant Daniel Murphey had dedi-
cated that time to emptying out the dating pools of
Hurlburt Field, Eglin Air Force Base, Fort Walton
Beach and Okaloosa County, and had been ready to
start working on the rest of northern Florida, when
Allison had suddenly reappeared in his life.

He might have told his buddies back on Silver
Team of Hurlburt Field's elite special operations
combat control squadron that he liked playing the
field, but he knew better. He had been trying to forget. Now that he and Allison had reconnected,
Danny was ready to chuck it all and do the church
and the little redbrick-house-and-white-picket-fence
thing.

He'd been certain that he was ready to settle down
two years ago, but Allison hadn't been. She'd wanted
a career, and he, as a special ops combat control op-
erator, could not envision his wife working. Men
were supposed to provide for their families, and their
wives were supposed to care for the home and their
children. What better way to demonstrate his love
than by wanting to provide for the woman he loved.

Allison hadn't seen it that way then, and it had
caused a rift they had been unable to close.

They had never been able to compromise, and

that one thing, for Allison, had been a deal breaker. She'd walked out on him, accepted a transfer and a promotion, and had not looked back.

Danny was sure that now, after two years apart, two years where he'd sown all the wild oats he'd wanted to and gained the reputation of ladies' man extraordinaire among the other members of his squadron, he and Allison would be able to compromise. He was okay with her working until the kids came along, and maybe when the kids were older and in school, she could go back. What woman wouldn't agree to that?

Allison shifted positions, giving Danny a tantalizing view of her ripe, full breasts. He could imagine his child, his son, suckling at her breasts, and the thought made his heart swell, as well as another part of his anatomy. He brushed a strand of her long, jet-black hair away from her face so he could gaze at her beauty. God, he could watch her all night and never be bored.

He'd always known that Allison was THE ONE. And this time, he was certain that she knew it, too.

As much as he wanted to wake her, to get down on bended knees right now to propose, he'd wait. He wanted everything to be perfect.

He'd ask her first thing in the morning.

This time he was going to do it right. And this time he was certain she'd say yes. "Allison Carter, I want you so much," Danny whispered into the darkness.

"I know you're gonna give in and let me take care of you."

He leaned over and dropped a light kiss on her soft, full lips, then he lay back against the pillows and drifted off into contented sleep to dream of what would be.

But, when he woke up…he was alone.

With *Hometown Honey* (#1068), Kara Lennox launches a new three-book series called BLOND JUSTICE about three women who were duped by the same con man and vow to get even. But many things can get in the way of a woman's revenge, and for Cindy Lefler, it's a gorgeous sheriff's deputy named Luke Rheems—a man who's more than willing to help her get back on her feet again. Watch for the other books in the series, *Downtown Debutante* (coming September 2005) and *Out of Town Bride* (December 2005). We know you're going to love these fast-paced, humorous stories!

"Only twelve thousand biscuits left to bake," Cindy Lefler said cheerfully as she popped a baking sheet into the industrial oven at the Miracle Café. Though she loved the smell of fresh-baked biscuits, she had grown weary of the actual baking. One time, she'd tried to figure out how many biscuits she'd baked in her twenty-eight years. It had numbered well into the millions.

"I wish you'd stop counting them down," grumbled

Tonya Dewhurst, who was folding silverware into paper napkins. She was the café's newest waitress, but Cindy had grown to depend on her very quickly. "You're the only one who's happy you're leaving."

"I'll come back to visit."

"You'll be too busy being Mrs. Dex Shalimar, lady of leisure," Tonya said dreamily. "You sure know how to pick husbands." Then she straightened. "Oh, gosh, I didn't mean that the way it sounded."

Cindy patted Tonya's shoulder. "It's okay, I know what you mean."

She still felt a pang over losing Jim, which was only natural, she told herself. The disagreement between her husband's truck and a freight train had happened only a year ago. But she *had* picked a good one when she'd married him. And she'd gotten just plain lucky finding Dex.

"It's almost six," Cindy said. "Would you unlock the front door and turn on the Open sign, please?" A couple of the other waitresses, Iris and Kate, had arrived and were going through their morning routines. Iris had worked at the café for more than twenty years, Kate almost as long.

Tonya smiled. "Sure. Um, Cindy, do you have a buyer for the café yet?"

"Dex says he has some serious nibbles."

"I just hope the new owner will let me bring Micton to work with me."

Cindy cringed every time she heard that name. Tonya had thought it was so cute, naming her baby with a combination of hers and her husband's names—Mick and Tonya. Micton. Yikes! It was the type of back-woods logic that made Cindy want to leave Cottonwood.

Customers were actually waiting in line when Tonya opened the door—farmers and ranchers, mostly, in jeans and overalls, Stetsons and gimme hats, here to get a hearty breakfast and exchange gossip. Cindy went to work on the Daily Specials chalkboard that was suspended high above the cash register.

"Morning, Ms. Cindy."

She very nearly fell off her stepladder. Still, she managed to very pleasantly say, "Morning, Luke." The handsome sheriff's deputy always unnerved her. He showed up at 6:10, like clockwork, five days a week, and ordered the same thing—one biscuit with honey and black coffee. But every single time she saw him sitting there at the counter, that knowing grin on his face, she felt a flutter of surprise.

Kate rushed over from clearing a table to pour Luke his coffee and take his order. The woman was in her sixties at least, but Cindy could swear Kate blushed as she served Luke. He just had that effect on women, herself included. Even now, when she was engaged—hell, even when she'd been *married* to a man she'd loved fiercely—just looking at Luke made her pulse quicken and her face warm.

HARLEQUIN®

AMERICAN *Romance*®

A new miniseries from

Leah Vale

The McCoys of Dependable, Missouri, have built
an astounding fortune and national reputation of
trustworthiness for their chain of general retail stores
with the corporate motto, "Don't Trust It If It's Not
The Real McCoy." Only problem is, the lone son and
heir to the corporate dynasty has never been trustworthy
where the ladies are concerned.

After he's killed by a grizzly bear while fly-fishing in Alaska
and his will is read, the truth comes out: Marcus McCoy
loved 'em and left 'em wherever he went. And now he's
acknowledging the offspring of his illicit liaisons!

THE BAD BOY (July 2004)
THE COWBOY (September 2004)
THE MARINE (March 2005)
THE RICH BOY (May 2005)

The only way to do the right thing and quell any
scandal that would destroy the McCoy empire is to
bring these lost millionaires into the fold....

Available wherever Harlequin Books are sold.

www.eHarlequin.com   HARTLM

If you enjoyed what you just read,
then we've got an offer you can't resist!

Take 2 bestselling
love stories FREE!
Plus get a FREE surprise gift!

Clip this page and mail it to Harlequin Reader Service®

IN U.S.A.	IN CANADA
3010 Walden Ave.	P.O. Box 609
P.O. Box 1867	Fort Erie, Ontario
Buffalo, N.Y. 14240-1867	L2A 5X3

YES! Please send me 2 free Harlequin American Romance® novels and my free surprise gift. After receiving them, if I don't wish to receive anymore, I can return the shipping statement marked cancel. If I don't cancel, I will receive 4 brand-new novels every month, before they're available in stores! In the U.S.A., bill me at the bargain price of $4.24 plus 25¢ shipping & handling per book and applicable sales tax, if any*. In Canada, bill me at the bargain price of $4.99 plus 25¢ shipping & handling per book and applicable taxes**. That's the complete price and a savings of at least 10% off the cover prices—what a great deal! I understand that accepting the 2 free books and gift places me under no obligation ever to buy any books. I can always return a shipment and cancel at any time. Even if I never buy another book from Harlequin, the 2 free books and gift are mine to keep forever.

154 HDN DZ7S
354 HDN DZ7T

Name	(PLEASE PRINT)	
Address	Apt.#	
City	State/Prov.	Zip/Postal Code

Not valid to current Harlequin American Romance® subscribers.

Want to try two free books from another series?
Call 1-800-873-8635 or visit www.morefreebooks.com.

* Terms and prices subject to change without notice. Sales tax applicable in N.Y.
** Canadian residents will be charged applicable provincial taxes and GST.
  All orders subject to approval. Offer limited to one per household.
  ® are registered trademarks owned and used by the trademark owner and or its licensee.

AMER04R   ©2004 Harlequin Enterprises Limited

e♦HARLEQUIN.com

The Ultimate Destination for Women's Fiction

The eHarlequin.com online community is *the* place to share opinions, thoughts and feelings!

- Joining the community is easy, fun and **FREE!**

- Connect with **other romance fans** on our message boards.

- Meet your **favorite authors** without leaving home!

- **Share opinions** on books, movies, celebrities…and *more!*

Here's what our members say:

"I love the friendly and helpful atmosphere filled with support and humor."
—Texanna (eHarlequin.com member)

"Is this the place for me, or what? There is nothing I love more than 'talking' books, especially with fellow readers who are reading the same ones I am."
—Jo Ann (eHarlequin.com member)

Join today by visiting
www.eHarlequin.com!

INTCOMM04R

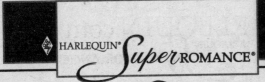

HARLEQUIN *Super*ROMANCE®

On sale May 2005

With Child by Janice Kay Johnson
(SR #1273)

All was right in Mindy Fenton's world when she went to bed one night. But before it was over everything had changed—and not for the better. She was awakened by Brendan Quinn with the news that her husband had been shot and killed. Now Mindy is alone and pregnant…and Quinn is the only one she can turn to.

On sale June 2005

Pregnant Protector by Anne Marie Duquette
(SR #1283)

Lara Nelson is a good cop, which is why she and her partner—a German shepherd named Sadie—are assigned to protect a fellow officer whose life is in danger. But as Lara and Nick Cantello attempt to discover who wants Nick dead, attraction gets the better of judgment, and in nine months there will be someone else to consider.

On sale July 2005

The Pregnancy Test by Susan Gable
(SR #1285)

Sloan Thompson has good reason to worry about his daughter once she enters her "rebellious" phase. And that's before she tells him she's pregnant. Then he discovers his own actions have consequences. This about-to-be grandfather is also going to be a father again.

Available wherever Harlequin books are sold.

www.eHarlequin.com   HSR9ML0405

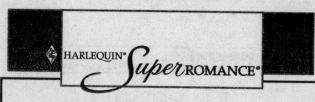

HARLEQUIN *Super*ROMANCE®

Come to Shelter Valley, Arizona, with
Tara Taylor Quinn...

...and with Caroline Prater, who's new to town. Caroline, from rural Kentucky, is a widow and a single mother.

She's also pregnant—after a brief affair with John Strickland, who lives in Shelter Valley.

And although she's always known she was adopted, Caroline's just discovered she has a twin sister she didn't know about. A twin who doesn't know about her. A twin who lives in Shelter Valley...and is a friend of John Strickland's.

Shelter Valley. Read the books. Live the life.

"Quinn writes touching stories about real people that transcend plot type or genre."
—Rachel Potter, *All About Romance*

www.eHarlequin.com   HSRSB0405

HARLEQUIN®

AMERICAN-*Romance*®

THE ABBOTTS
A Dynasty in the Making

A series by
Muriel Jensen

The Abbotts of Losthampton, Long Island, first settled in New York back in the days of the *Mayflower*.

Now they're a power family, owning one of the largest business conglomerates in the country.

But…appearances can be deceiving.

HIS FAMILY
May 2005

Campbell Abbott should have been thrilled when his little sister, abducted at the age of fourteen months, returns to the Abbott family home. Instead, he finds her…annoying. After a DNA test proves she isn't his long-lost sister, he suddenly realizes where his prickly attitude toward her comes from—and admits he'll do anything to ensure she stays in his family now.

Read about the Abbotts:

HIS BABY (May 2004)
HIS WIFE (August 2004)
HIS FAMILY (May 2005)
HIS WEDDING (September 2005)

Available wherever Harlequin books are sold.

HARLEQUIN®

AMERICAN Romance®

Blond Justice

Betrayed…and betting on each other.

Coming in May 2005, don't miss the first book in

Kara Lennox's

brand-new miniseries.

HOMETOWN HONEY

Harlequin American Romance #1067

Cindy Lefler gets the shock of her life when her groom-to-be leaves her just days before their pending nuptials. But rather than get mad, Cindy plans to get even. And thanks to two other jilted brides and one very sexy local sheriff named Luke Rheemes, Cindy soon smells victory for her and her little boy. And maybe even her own happily-ever-after?

DOWNTOWN DEBUTANTE
(September 2005)

OUT OF TOWN BRIDE
(December 2005)

Available wherever Harlequin books are sold.

www.eHarlequin.com   HARHH0505